ON THE MAP

MILE HIGH STALLIONS
BOOK 1

CHRISTINA HOVLAND

For rights information, please contact:
Prospect Agency
551 Valley Road, PMB 377
Upper Montclair, NJ 07043
(718) 788-3217

Cover Design: Christina Hovland

This book was originally put on pre-order as
The Accidental Bride.

For the pop star in all of us.

CHAPTER ONE

MAYA

"Hot damn, I'm back." My great Sin City Time-Out had ended.

I flicked my wrist, popping on a dose of mascara for night number one of the girls' vacation. Hell, I may not have had the best track record with all things Nevada, but if there was one tidbit I'd learned in life—it was to keep trying until I got it right.

I did a lot of trying, since getting it right was more elusive than I'd ever expected.

Someday, I'd move up from being a backup singer to become an a-list headliner, have my own manager, with a career that finally took off. Someday, however, had yet to happen. No matter how hard I tried.

But I was in Vegas to push it forward.

Make it happen *and* have a kickass weekend of fun.

Tonight, I would attend the engagement party for one of my childhood friends. Bonus, one of his cousins was a big deal in the music industry and, rumor had it, that cousin was slated to be at the party.

That was the main reason I'd broken my exile. Since my last

Las Vegas marriage that ended in divorce two years ago, I'd avoided this city.

But I'd done my time away, and now I was ready to roll. A brief ha-cha-cha dance was the only shimmy-hop my gold-sequined tube dress would allow. Oh hells yes, I was ba-a-ack.

I was back, and I looked amazing, so I took that opportunity to prop my cell on a nearby shelf and sing a few bars of Mariah Carey, ensuring I hit a fantastic whistle note.

I checked the reel and then posted to my socials.

I wasn't sure why I kept sending content online when the only ones who interacted were my fellow back-up singers, friends, sisters, and... Mom. Dad would've thrown me a like or two, but he didn't do social media.

"I'm so glad you came home for this." My friend Angela slipped into the room beside me and peered into the mirror. She ran her fingernail along the crease where her lips met in the middle so she could fix the lipstick smudge without having to reapply the whole shebang. The shade of Heartbreak Pink I'd snagged for her at an airport kiosk was the perfect complement to her blond hair and blue eyes.

Angela would say her cheeks were too round, her ass too big, and her skin too pale, but the entire package came together to create an innocent schoolgirl look that was catnip to most members of the male species.

I often reminded her how amazing she was both aesthetically and, more importantly, as a person.

"You know I couldn't miss this," I said.

Angela gave me a look like my martini was missing an olive. Short explanation? The last two times I'd been home, I'd intentionally gotten sloshed and unintentionally gotten married.

What could I say? I used to believe in love at first sight. Turned out that I used to love the idea of love, but I stunk at the actual carry through. I'd realized by this point that love had little to do with long-term relationships. Not for me, anyway.

None of that mattered now, since I was here to make connections.

A connection.

That major connection that would propel me forward and put me on the map.

"Oh, come on." Angela hip bumped me. "You're going to get frown lines. You can't be sad in Vegas. It's not allowed."

"No, I know." I tried not to frown, but the smile felt forced.

"I heard that Jared's fiancée is actually pretty great," Angela said, clearly trying to change the subject.

As happy as I felt for my friend getting engaged and having a party before getting married, I was mildly down that so many of my friends had found their future and lived it, while I remained stuck in the mud, chasing dreams that never came true.

Still a backup singer for those in the spotlight and still very, very single.

Our more responsible friend, Emily—the one with the voice of reason—sauntered into the room.

"Our one rule is... what?" she asked.

No one answered. Not because we didn't know, but the question sounded rhetorical.

"The one rule we set?" Emily paused again, clearly waiting for Angela or me to respond.

Right, so clearly, this wasn't a pretend test. Of course, I knew the rule since I was the reason for the aforementioned rule: don't get lit, get married, or bring husband number three back to the condo.

"No strangers at the house," I replied, mimicking the same tone as Emily. "No one comes home with us. And by us, we're referring to me." I pointed to myself. "Not to worry, I'm here to make connections, not meet a man."

Ahem. However...

That didn't mean I couldn't find a nice palate cleanser from my most recent boyfriend *if* the opportunity presented itself.

Because that most recent boyfriend of mine? He'd already moved on to Little Miss Perfect.

"I think you should wear your Vegas Bride badge with pride and go for a third husband." Angela finished with her makeup, popping the cap back on her setting spray. "I mean, let's make the trip worth it."

"Cute, but absolutely not," I replied.

There was no way—none—that I would end my twenties with another failed marriage.

If I ever got married again, I wanted a handsome fiancé, lots of chemistry, a four-tier cake, to be married under the stars in the summer, with a jazz band and a pasta bar with six kinds of sauce.

According to the math—since it was already summer—I'd need to be engaged for a minimum of six months to get the full bridal experience. All that to say, my next wedding was at least a year away.

"Third husband. Third husband," Angela chanted.

"On this point, we disagree, Ang," Emily said.

She wasn't fussing with her makeup because, honestly? She didn't have to.

Emily's tan skin, black hair, and bone structure mirrored what most women desperately tried to achieve through copious amounts of contouring and highlighting. She also stood impressively tall but wasn't afraid to rock stilettos when the occasion called for them.

Occasions like tonight.

I aspired to be more like Emily. A woman ready to flip the calendar on her twenties should have more to show for it than two failed marriages, a job that wasn't totally awful, a kick-ass manicure, and more good hair days than bad.

Emily had the luck in life that would've made me jealous, had I not understood how she worked her tush off to make all that good stuff happen. Case in point? When Jared announced the party plans, Emily jumped to call her uncle about borrowing his condo.

Then she wrangled and finagled until she had her girls on an excellent-priced flight, non-stop to Vegas.

Make no mistake: this trip didn't happen to Emily. It happened because of her.

"Maya," Emily said. "I just don't want you to get hurt, that's all."

That was sweet. Really, it was.

"Well, don't worry. I won't bring anyone here, either," Angela said, raising her right hand like she was swearing in to testify.

Angela was queen of the friend zone with men. She was the bomb at the catch and release game, accomplishing it with practiced ease and remarkable skill.

Most guys checked out after a breakup, but not with Angela. With Angela, they stuck around to be her friend.

For real, they called her for advice and everything.

She'd even taught me a few tricks that helped during the annulment and the...uh...divorce. Was it hot in here? My neck was warmer, that's for sure.

"Then it's agreed." Emily snatched her purse and rummaged through, doing her last-minute did-I-get-everything check. "Ready?"

Emily held her hand out, palm down. We both added ours to the stack.

"Ready," everyone said in near unison.

Here's the deal. Emily was a life planner, extreme. But once we roamed wild in Vegas, things went...well...differently. We all believed that the Sin City experience was a helluva lot more fun when the plan came to us, instead of vice versa.

Though I did question that rationale, given my history.

My phone rang. I glanced at the screen.

"Ten bucks says it's her mom," Emily said.

Unfortunately, she wasn't wrong.

"Hi, Mom," I said, moving to the living room, so the girls didn't have to listen to whatever tear she would go on. "What's up?"

5

"You're in Nevada," Mom announced, like I didn't know where I was.

"I am." Was I sweating? A little, yes. I...er...hadn't mentioned the trip to my mother.

"You and Nevada are ammonia and bleach." Mom clicked her tongue like she did when she got worried. "This is a bad idea."

I opened my mouth to respond, but Mom got there first. So instead, I distracted myself by mentally rearranging the couch so it would work more functionally with the coffee table. Six inches over, and that coffee table wouldn't be in the flow of foot traffic from the kitchen.

Mom continued talking, but I blocked her out, electing to reconsider the placement of the Elvis figurines instead.

The condo held an entire Elvis collection—from itty bitty dime-sized statues all the way to a life-size art deco bust.

The bust perched on top of one of the Grecian columns near the flat screen. I traced along the pompadour with my index finger instead of focusing on Mom's breakdown of my last Vegas encounter and how it had ended with a divorce. I turned Elvis a few degrees to the left, so he wasn't looking straight in the guest bathroom. The King didn't need to always face the throne. No indeed.

Mom stopped long enough to catch her breath, so I took that as my opportunity to pause and reassure her.

"I promise, I'm going to behave." I had a one-drink maximum, and then I was on club soda for the rest of the night. "I'm here for business." Mostly.

"It's not you I worry about. It's the men who don't respect you," Mom huffed.

"I really don't want to have this conversation right now," I said. Or ever.

"A conversation about the abundance of respect you should demand from the opposite sex?" Mom asked, all baloney innocence.

I didn't like it when Mom threw around the sex word, because it made me itchy all over. But since she brought it up…

"There are times in a woman's life when she simply wants to be respected for the things she's accomplished," I said. "And there are times she'd prefer that respect served with a side of tongue and heavy petting." That was the truth.

This was the problem with my latest ex-boyfriend. The guy was nice as could be and boring as rice cakes both in life and… in bed. Which was why it smarted that he'd been the one to break it off when he met the perfect woman for him. Of course, he'd waited until after I scooted his bedroom furniture around and fit everything where it should go for better energy flow.

That was okay, though; he and his new girlfriend and his bedroom furniture didn't matter. All the history was safely tucked away in my memories, and today was another step toward the future.

Mom let out a deep sigh that implied this conversation was only beginning. "Honey, with all the love in the world, I have to beg you to leave Las Vegas before things… happen."

"Nothing is gonna happen," I assured.

We were going to be late for the party. I didn't want to be late. So I did a bad thing. I pretended I couldn't hear Mom anymore, so she would hang up.

Of course, I knew this was my mom. Mom, who sacrificed for me and was in labor for sixteen hours before I arrived.

She made this point a lot.

But I wouldn't do anything she needed to panic about.

On that note, my little "can't hear you" trick worked, and she hung up. Then I slipped my cell into my purse, grabbed my bolero satin jacket, and turned to get my girls.

Except the front door to the condo was open, and a man stood in the doorway with three oversized suitcases.

My pulse paused. Straight up, it glitched.

I wasn't a screamer, but I made an interestingly surprised meep noise. He didn't seem nefarious, what with all the luggage and the fact he had a key in his hand.

Still, the guy stared at me like I'd grown an extra couple of limbs out of my head. Probably the respect with tongue thing I'd said to Mom. I wouldn't have said that if I'd known I had an audience.

At that point, I should've said something to him. That would've been the logical thing to do when a man dressed in flannel stood there. Instead, I took a step backward. Unfortunately, this caused me to trip on the edge of the rug.

The rug placement was total shit.

Damn, damn, damn, that little trip had me bumping right into the Elvis bust. He tipped forward. I turned to grab him, and his face pressed right on up against my breasts.

Elvis, not the guy at the door.

I made an oomph sound while the ghost of Elvis himself seemed to embody my mother's words, ensuring that things I didn't want to happen would happen. Oh, yes, the King of Rock 'n Roll motorboated my girls and continued to tilt precariously forward.

That plaster Elvis was heavy. Like stupid heavy.

"Help me," I said in a panic, to McFlannel.

Doing my best to get Elvis back on the stand wasn't enough, because he seemed extremely attached to my boobs. The tube top? No longer a great idea.

CHAPTER
TWO

MAYA

McFlannel dropped his bags at the door, which was unfortunate because he'd have to pick them right back up when he left, but it was also fortunate because he took four long strides to me and helped wrangle Elvis back where he belonged.

He seemed to be actively avoiding looking my way.

"Holy crap." I checked my top. It was a close one, but no nip slip. "That would've been awful, huh?"

He made a noncommittal noise in the back of his throat that could've been an agreement or disagreement. It was hard to tell.

Thankfully, the girls remained safely enclosed in the elastic and satin top. Then I slid my gaze from Elvis—he was fine—to McFlannel.

The guy didn't have any serial killer vibes, as I was fairly certain serial killers didn't bring luggage with them. Also, I didn't think I'd ever been attracted to a serial killer before, and here I was, dancing along the edge of sunstroke from how hot this guy was. Hot in all the hunky sense.

"Uh. Thank you for your help." I stepped back a smidge. "Also, who are you?"

The guy looked like he honest-to-God worked outside with his hands.

"Who are you?" he asked, laidback, like I hadn't just posed that exact query. "Are you supposed to be here?"

Again, wasn't that my line?

"Yes, and I'm Maya." I shouldn't just toss my name out like that to random people I didn't know. And, also, I should have gotten Emily and let her deal with whatever was happening here, but I didn't. Probably because of hot lumberjack guy fumes messing with my brainwaves.

"Look. I'm not sure what's going on." He sort of tilted his head to the side. "Elliott will be right up. It's his aunt's place."

"You're here with Elliott?" I asked in horror, because that was about the worst news I'd heard in forever.

"You know him?"

Of course, I knew Elliott. "He's Emily's brother."

He was a sports agent. Which meant...

"Are you a football player?"

He frowned. "Maybe."

This guy, as a football player, made so much sense. And it helped to disperse those hot guy fumes he'd had before. I didn't have a great history with football players. Not since my first boyfriend made the varsity team when we were in high school.

"Maybe isn't really an answer," I pointed out, with the little eyebrow quirk I'd perfected by practicing in the mirror with my hairbrush microphone.

"Yeah. I play. But... I'm not really into broadcasting that right now. I'm supposed to be incognito this weekend."

"Ah," I said.

He stood there, crossing his arms.

I stood there, too, crossing my arms.

"Elliott is parking the car," McFlannel said, after the awkward pause dragged on a few beats too long.

I peeked around him. "Are these suitcases all yours?"

He blinked way harder than necessary. "No."

Right, well… "Then who do they belong to?"

"Elliott." He gave me a look like some of the cheese had slid off my cracker. "I lost the…you know…never mind."

"You lost the…?" I asked.

"Doesn't matter." He shook his head. "I said I'd bring them up."

"Oh," I said.

"Okay."

We stood there in an odd sort of silence.

"I lost a bet," he said, finally.

Well, that made more sense.

I refused to check him out again because this was my first night back, and I couldn't just pick up the first guy I ran into. And definitely not a football player. Of all the players, they were the worst.

Except… I hated to say this, but this guy felt different. Different in a fantastic way.

He did the thing guys do where they check out a woman and their eyes flare only around the edges to show their bodies are interested, even if their mind hasn't quite caught up with the physical response.

You know what? Actually, there wasn't a rule or anything about picking up the first guy I ran into.

This was Vegas. The one place rules were bendable.

No! Bad Maya! Stop it!

I was in town for business. This man was not business.

Then again… business wouldn't take all night.

I peeked to ensure my maybe future one-night stand wasn't wearing a wedding band or showing the pale line of a guy who had slipped one off.

No ring. No pale line.

"Maya," he said my name like he was doing a taste test at an ice cream shop. Savoring the vowels to see how they felt against his tongue. "I like your name, Maya."

He may as well have licked me with the way my body got all kinds of goosebumps.

"You haven't mentioned your name," I pointed out.

He heaved a deep breath. "Sloan."

"Sloan-n-n Stevens?" I asked.

Not that I followed football, but I followed TMZ, and they devoted an entire section on last week's breakdown to Sloan Stevens and the way he fumbled endorsements.

"You play center for the Denver Stallions." I remembered his position because it was right in the middle. Ba-dum-bum.

I smiled at my own inside joke.

He nodded. "That's me."

He frowned, and the thin little wire that had been snapping and sizzling between us was no longer.

That was a freaking bummer.

"Out of curiosity, how much of what I said, uh, before on the phone, did you hear?" I asked. "Did you hear the part about..." Er... what was the best way to phrase this?

"Respect being served with a side of tongue? Yeah, I heard that part, Maya." Again, he did the taste test thing with my name. Dammit all, I still liked it.

Perhaps that little sizzle was still a live wire.

"Are you still talking to your mom—" Emily came to a halt behind me. Well, I assumed Emily stopped moving because she didn't show up in front of me, but I felt her presence there.

Which was good, because Elliott stepped right through the doorway like the Las Vegas killjoy he was.

Same as his sister, he had tan skin, dark hair, and loads of height. Unlike Emily, he hadn't coordinated with their uncle about using the condo for the weekend.

"You cannot be here," Emily said, holding up her hand and silently snarling in that sweet way little sisters did to their big brothers.

Elliott ignored the snarl as he took in the situation, pausing briefly on me and then a touch longer on Angela. Probably because of the pink lipstick—it worked that well on her. I made a mental note to buy extra tubes for her birthday.

"What're you doing here?" he countered, stepping into the room with another guy not far behind.

"Uncle Milo lent me the condo." Emily blinked hard, as though it would help make her point.

Elliott pulled a face. "Aunt Lisa said I could borrow the condo."

"Well, crud, this is no good," I said, hoping that might help slice up the tension into bite-size pieces. Blah. No matter how I sliced it, this scenario was unfortunate.

"Aunt Lisa gave us a key. We're not leaving," Elliott announced, already making himself at home on the sofa.

Uncle Milo and Aunt Lisa weren't exactly known for their communication skills. I understood this because Emily, Angela, and I all spent loads of time together growing up, which meant family for one was family for all. Huzzah!

Of course, that meant everyone had a right to be in the space, and, it seemed, no one had a right to be there. Except the Elvis figurines.

The brother and sister began their standoff, even though everyone knew Emily would win. Elliott may have had the edge of negotiating for a living, but Emily had sibling law on her side. That law being that she was there first.

"Are we staying?" guy number three asked. A man with California tanned skin in a pressed polo shirt, slacks, and glasses I'd bet were only for style. He got a kick out of the brother and sister deadlock.

"Who are you?" Emily asked.

"Finn," he said.

"Finn Taylor?" Angela said, pouting her pink lips like a lusty bunny in his direction.

He nodded.

"He plays offense," Angela loud whispered to the rest of us.

"Ladies. Nice to meet you all." Finn acted like the brother-sister standoff wasn't happening and greeted each of us with a nod.

"Uncle Milo gave me the code to get in." Emily kept her tone even.

"And Aunt Lisa gave me the key to get in," her brother countered in his 'I'm Elliott, mega-big-deal-sports-agent' tone.

The guy seriously needed to scarf a fistful of chill pills and pull the stick out of his—

"We were here first," Emily clarified. Honestly, she wasn't wrong. If possession was nine-tenths of the law, then we owned the joint. Which was why she'd win the argument.

"And we aren't leaving." Elliott crossed his arms.

Well, damn. That made it harder for everyone and quite the pickle.

Sloan let out a deeply annoyed breath. I could see why he'd be annoyed after the way TMZ slaughtered him, and now, he was without a place to stay in Vegas. His facial hair probably itched, too.

This wasn't going anywhere quickly, so I looked at Sloan instead of listening to the brother and sister argue.

Not gonna lie. I licked my lips. Then I immediately stopped because even if he looked like a snack, I didn't want to have to fix my lip gloss.

"No," Emily said, louder. "We've got plans. Go check in at a hotel."

"Not happening." Elliott shook his head. "I booked the condo. We're staying here."

He must've realized he might not win this battle because his voice got higher pitched at the end. Emily would snag onto that weakness, figuratively grab him by the scruff of his neck, and shake him around until he cried...well...Uncle Milo.

"Maybe see if Mom and Dad will let you stay with them?" Emily made a sucks-for-you-but-doesn't-really-suck-for-me expression.

"There's plenty of room," Angela said, chiming in from behind Emily with her perfected chirpy sunshine and a sly glance at Finn.

Elliott grumbled like a storm cloud at that, which was silly because Angela gave him what he wanted.

"We can share," I said with a shrug. There actually was space.

Four whole bedrooms. They'd have to bunk up, but there was plenty of sleeping area.

"I don't mind sharing," Angela added with a heavy dose of her pink smile.

Was it me or did Elliott's eyes darken a teensy tiny touch at the smile?

"I mind," he said, his jaw ticcing as he clenched his teeth.

Right, clearly, this wouldn't be easy. It never was with him.

Whatever. I had been in time-out entirely too long, and that exile ended now. No way would I spend my night here watching this nonsense when I had a city to paint red.

"Look." I gestured to the living room. "It's not like we're going to be here very much. It's Vegas, and there are cocktails to drink, poker to play, and shows to see." I paused and made jazz hands. "Let's get to it."

"My stuff's already in the blue bedroom," Emily said, brushing past her brother. "Angela's across the hall, and Maya's next to her. You all can use the other room."

Elliott made a *pf-shaw* sound.

"Not to worry. We all know that after three lemon drops, she'll sleep anywhere. I'll have her bunk with me," Angela said to Elliott, following Emily.

"There are lemon drops?" Elliott somehow asked the innocent question and said it was a bad idea all at once.

"Not for me," I assured him. "One cocktail, and I'm done tonight."

"Do you ladies feel like some company?" Finn asked, rubbing his palms together as a slow grin spread. "I have a feeling we'll have more fun with you around."

How was that even a question? Moving on…

"You guys should come with us," Angela said.

Emily stared death daggers at her.

"They said we should bring plus-ones." Angela held her ground against Emily's attitude.

"Will there be food?" Sloan asked, all casual-like, but with the underlying intensity of a guy who appreciated a good steak.

I moved beside him and lifted my hand as though painting a gorgeous picture full of happy accidents. "There will be entire buffets."

He gave me a funny look, but his eyes lingered a touch too long as the edges of his lips twitched.

On that thought, Emily cleared her throat.

Maybe we had been staring at each other entirely too long.

"If there are lemon drops, we're in. I'm keeping an eye on you." Elliott ran his hand over his face. "I thought I only had to watch out for Sloan this weekend."

"Your weekend just got busy," Angela announced all cheery.

Elliott practically turned into a puppy running circles at her feet.

"If there's food, I'm in." Sloan followed Finn in Emily's wake, his gaze pausing on me and raising my blood pressure just a smidge.

I was so twitterpated, I nearly followed him without thinking.

But wait, he couldn't just go out in Vegas dressed like that, could he?

"Hold up," I said, loud enough to get everyone's attention.

"Yeah?" Sloan asked.

Flannel was nice and all, but this was Vegas, in the summer, and we were going clubbing. So what, I couldn't have those lemon drops or the history of poor decisions that came with them? I could still get my dance on.

"Don't you want to change or something?" I asked.

Sloan glanced down at the button-up shirt. "What's wrong with what I'm wearing?"

"Uh…" Technically, nothing. But it was hot as balls out there.

You know what, though? This was a problem for the future.

"Nothing." I gestured him out. "Let's find that buffet."

CHAPTER
THREE

SLOAN

Not only had I screwed up, ran my mouth, and lost another endorsement deal, but the promise of a buffet hadn't happened. Loads of booze with an open bar, sure. But not even a bowl of rolls to be found.

Not to say I got grumpy when my blood sugar dropped low, but I didn't get happy, that's for damn sure.

Especially when my phone kept dinging from my teammates checking in and inadvertently reminding me of my fuckup with the ZipZing sports drink brand.

All I did was mention that there was a "fuck-ton" of sugar in their beverages. Turned out, fuck-ton wasn't a unit of measurement this brand liked to have associated with their brand. So, instead of letting me correct my mistake, they cut me loose as a brand ambassador and paused all sponsorship chatter with the Stallions marketing department.

Coach told me to, and I'm quoting, "Get the hell out of his town for a while."

A crew of servers went through the room, offering appetizers. Unfortunately, the small plops of unicorn fluff did nothing to satiate any hunger from missing lunch because I was getting chewed out by my coach.

The anxiety of being in the twilight of my football career, paired with this current disaster, with the bonus of being hungry, made me twitchy.

But there was Maya—a bright spot in a day of total bullshit.

Maya, with her brown hair and brown eyes, stepped up to the DJ booth and snatched the microphone. The music stopped, and the DJ tilted his chin to her.

"I have a pre-wedding present for Jared and Jamie," she said into the microphone. "I hope you like it."

And with that, using her palms, she tapped out a rhythm on the side of the booth that sounded oddly familiar, but not something I could put my finger on.

The DJ continued clapping to the beat as Maya went into an a cappella version of Ingrid Michaelson's, *The Way I Am*.

When she got to the part about Rogaine and hair loss, the soon-to-be bride plastered herself to the groom, and he kissed the hell out of her.

Maya smiled and got more into the song, her eyes catching mine and...fuck all...then she sang the song to me. Her voice was light as angel food cake, but somehow still strong as steel—a combination I was certain I'd never heard before.

A combination I seriously dug.

With the song finished, she did a shimmy shake, and I couldn't stop grinning like an idiot. Grinning and clapping along with everyone else as Maya took a cute little bow and handed back the mic.

Me? Still fucking grinning.

"You look like the opposite of miserable." Finn sat beside me on the long bench looking over the club and handed me a sushi spoon with more airy fluff pseudo-food.

I ate the fluff—it tasted like chicken-flavored cotton candy threads. Definitely not a flavor-texture combination I'd ever endorse.

Then again, given my current situation, I'd have to endorse it so I didn't lose my house.

Maya needed to sing another song or something, because the chicken threads totally wrecked my happy of moments before.

"Elliott finally manage to get you that meeting with ZipZing?" Finn asked, serious as a timeout in overtime.

I shook my head. "No luck."

"You notice that the food here is... not food?" Finn asked around another chicken fluff bite.

"I'm starving, man," I said to Finn. "I'd settle for crappy pizza. Or the cardboard box it arrived in."

Maya glanced my way, snagged my gaze, and grinned at me from the edge of the dance party. That was an invitation if I'd ever seen one.

Finn glanced between me and Maya. "You really into her?"

I gave him a *yeah, so?* Nod.

Finn pulled his lips to the side. "Just..." He thought way too hard about what he would say next. "You left Denver, so Coach wouldn't murder you for doing something stupid. That woman there? Well, from the way you're looking at her? You'll do something stupid."

I didn't know what to say to that. So instead, I said—

"You should get drunk, don't you think?"

By him, I think I meant me. I... I should get drunk. Take this opportunity to use tequila to forget all about my fuckups.

I got ready to stand. Figured I'd head Maya's way, offer to take her to buy food not made from threads and air. She snipped those plans in two by sauntering toward me, hips swaying, eyes sparkling.

Finn raised his eyebrows. "You're gonna go be stupid."

I glared at my friend and pretended to throw a football straight at his face.

Maya's friend walked to us right alongside her. This one was... Emily. Yeah, Elliott's sister.

"Dance with me, Finn?" Emily asked, holding out her hand.

Finn didn't hesitate, taking Emily's hand and heading into the pit of people.

"Hey," Maya said, looking up at me from under those long eyelashes of hers.

My body heated under her gaze. Uh-huh, she made that happen with only a look.

"Hey," I replied. The only thing that seemed to exist was me and her and whatever the spark was between us. That was a new sensation now, wasn't it?

"Want to sit?" I asked, stumbling over the last syllable.

She nodded, pulling her bottom lip between her teeth. Just like that, the heat from before flared again.

I wasn't much for making lists, not really. But if I were, and I started a list of attributes I dug, the lip thing would be right at the top.

I sat. She sat.

Then she crossed her legs toward me and even though it was loud, I swear I could hear the sound of skin on skin as her thighs brushed. My blood thrummed hotter, and my stomach paused its chewing on itself. It didn't have blood anymore to feed that desire, not with all of it currently pooling elsewhere...

"They should serve actual food at these things," she said—shouted—over the bass.

"I'd take a pizza right about now," I agreed.

She laughed at that. "It should be a requirement at all events. Feed us."

"Your song was gorgeous," I said, meaning it.

She lifted her shoulder. Frowned. "Eh."

Now, that? That surprised me.

"I'm serious," I said. "You've got a gift."

"Well, thank you," she said, her cheeks getting pink.

I moved closer to her space, so we didn't have to shout. Maya smelled like cherries with a hint of vanilla. I'd always liked cherries.

Bass bumped, lights flashed, and the party continued around

us. But when she leaned into my space, I didn't care about anything other than what she would say next.

"It's weird, you know?" she said, lips right up against my ear.

I didn't know. Not at all.

She caught my vibe because she continued, "Watching people move on with their lives in such great ways. Like Jared getting married. Emily making partner at her firm. Angela planning her solo trip to Munich just because she wants to. Meanwhile, I'm walking in circles. Same ol', same ol'." She glanced down at her hands, then socked me in the stomach with her gaze. "I didn't even get to meet the *one* person I came to see. She didn't show up to the party, so now I have to stalk her at the wedding. You know what I mean?"

I didn't know. Not really. But—

"My dad always said that nothing matters if you don't acknowledge the effort you put in. Maybe, just let yourself be happy you're here," I suggested. "You showed up."

She blushed and glanced to her hands in her lap.

I opened my mouth to say something else I hoped might be brilliant. Instead, Maya's gaze slid to someone else behind me. Before I could open my mouth, Maya said, "Well, shit."

Her focus went one hundred percent to whatever was behind me.

Why did I suddenly feel like I'd forgotten to put on clothes before coming to the party? Losing Maya's attention made the room colder. Made me feel… naked.

Maya stood; her eyes were wide. "Why are you here?"

I craned my neck to get a look at who she'd addressed. A guy in a suit grinned at her and reached for her to pull her into a hug.

She dodged.

I had no claim on her—zero. None. But now, I felt awfully protective. I didn't snarl or growl, but something inside me wanted to.

"Family friend of the bride," the guy said.

Maya stepped slightly away from him, cutting a glance at me

with a flare in her eyes that seemed to be a request. Whatever it was, let's be honest, I'd do it.

Maya pulled her bottom lip between her teeth again. She was nervous.

Good to know: Maya gnawed on her lip when she got nervous. I noted it. Tucked the tidbit of knowledge away in my pocket.

"Can you believe all this?" A brown-haired woman slid her arm into the crook of the suit guy's elbow. "They went all out with this party."

"This is my wife," the guy said, and Maya paled.

"Sherry," the woman said, pointing to herself.

"Hi." Maya flashed a kind of genuine smile that I would've bought without hesitation, except for the little concerned lines that etched around the edges of her eyelids and the way she darted her eyes just a tad too quickly between the two of them. Maya glanced at me again, as though searching for that help.

Honest as all hell, I didn't know what was going on with this, but instinct took over, and I stood, moving closer to Maya like I had her back. I didn't mind it, because I did have her back. Though I hadn't one iota of an idea of why she needed me.

Suit guy finally looked my way. "Who's this?"

I stood a little taller, like a guy did when he sensed a chub-measuring competition about to be thrown his direction.

Maya didn't answer the question about who I was, which was a bummer because I kinda wanted to hear her answer.

"I'm whoever Maya needs me to be," I heard myself say.

She pulled at her bottom lip again in a total disruption to any thought processes happening in my brain.

Damn, but I hated that I liked when she did that. Didn't matter though; I was a good guy who was also starving.

"You ready to hit up that buffet you promised me?" I asked, tilting my thumb toward the exit.

The tense lines around Maya's eyes finally relaxed.

CHAPTER
FOUR

MAYA

Sloan hadn't said a word about Dan, but it was clear he had questions brewing behind those brown eyes of his. Anyone would have questions, I understood that.

But he was patient. Didn't say a thing. And that drove me absolutely batshit crazy.

The restaurant we headed toward was just past the M&M Store. Sloan promised he'd been there before, and the food didn't include chicken broth thready things.

So we walked, and Sloan took in the sights. His arm brushed mine when we'd get jostled by the melee of people pushing brochures to pedestrians, smacking them against their hands to get attention, and occasionally shoving them right in our path.

Through it all, as we dodged them, Sloan said nothing.

Nada.

Not a thing.

He said nothing until I couldn't take any more nothing.

"Dan is my ex-husband," I said in a rush, without even a hitch to my step as we continued our trek past the M&M Store. "We were married for an entire two weeks before…"

How did one say, *He served me with divorce papers?* I mean, it didn't quite have a nice ring to it, did it now?

"Before we ended it," I said instead.

That sounded much more reasonable.

I mean, I did have to sign the divorce papers, too, so I was involved.

Sloan slowed, and he looked at me as we walked. Which was dangerous; he might walk into a pole or something. But he also played football, so he probably had excellent spatial awareness.

He held his hand out between us. I took it. He squeezed it.

While the mechanics of the motions were nothing special, there was something keenly sweet about the gesture.

"Then I'm glad we got you out of there," he said, loud enough to be heard over the general noise of Vegas at night.

My heart glitched the tiniest of beats at his words.

He didn't ask questions. Didn't push to know more.

That was…that was…well, dammit, that was nice.

It was nice to have someone not question every part of my history or try to project it into my future.

The crowds got intense outside the M&M Store with a celebrity sighting. It wasn't a Sloan sighting—though I would bet had anyone realized who he was, it would've only added to the chaos.

We did our best to scuttle through on our hunt for food that wasn't candy-coated chocolate pellets.

We had nearly—by mere inches—made it through the throng outside the store when I got distracted by the guy who looked exactly like the lead from the new blockbuster *Tarzan and Jane* movie.

While the celebrity wasn't Cher, Sloan and I still ended up in the mosh pit of fans.

"Sloan? Sloan Stevens!?" someone called. Sloan glanced in that direction and in only a matter of seconds, I promptly got shoved out of the way.

Sloan did reach for me, but he was too late. Which was how I found myself tangled in a gaggle of arms and legs. I deftly dodged the lady in pink stripes, nearly going down. For cripes' sake, there was no escape. The heel on my right boot caught the edge of the sidewalk and snapped.

With that, I clenched my back teeth, mentally cursing my lack of balance; it was easier than cursing about everyone on earth moving forward successfully with their lives while I stayed stuck walking in circles.

Stuck in all the ways. Currently unable to escape a celebrity sighting and pissed about the boots. Oddly choked up that this would be my last outing with this footwear. It probably had nothing to do with the boots, but still... damn. I loved them. Maybe I could salvage—

The crowd swarmed around me... Nope. There was no going back for the heel.

The whole scenario was more nerve wracking than the time I tried bangs three summers ago and then attempted to grow them long without barrettes. I might dream of being a pop princess, but I was still a girl who couldn't pull off bangs. That lesson was well and truly learned.

An elbow nearly clocked me in the temple. I scooted out of the way, ducking to maneuver out of the crowd. Maybe if I went down, I could crawl out. Stop, drop, and roll. Or was that only for fires?

If I dropped, I might not get the chance to roll. I could end up trampled, and that'd be worse than losing the boots, and Sloan wouldn't get his dinner.

But I'd lost him in the fray. There was no Sloan around now.

I tried to get on my tippy toes to see him, but no dice. Drat, this wasn't fun. I should've ordered my singular lemon drop martini, enjoyed it, gone back to the condo, and ordered a pizza.

Honestly, I would forego a martini and settle for one of the kitschy yardstick margaritas.

A calloused hand brushed against my elbow, gently gripping my arm and removing me from the fray. For some reason, this didn't scare the shit out of me.

I glanced up, up, up into Sloan's brown eyes.

"You good?" he asked. He'd dropped his hand once my extraction was complete. Still, he looked me over, checking for any damage.

That was nice. Not invasive.

Honestly, never in my life had I been so relieved to see a football player. Wasn't that a thought I never thought I'd think?

"Sloan." I blew out a breath. "You found me."

"I did."

Well, wasn't he just my knight in shining Pendleton?

Even being recognized by a handful of people, with his size and his demeanor, the guy had become a crowd deterrent. Even those who clearly recognized him weren't making a peep about it. I swore he growled low enough that everyone avoided our vicinity. And with me tucked safely into his personal space bubble, the crowd seemed to part around us.

"You hurt?" he asked, glancing over me as he spoke and seriously giving me goosebumps with the way his gaze trailed over my skin.

"No." I frowned at my heel-less boot. "Just my footwear." My kitten heel, white leather, pointed toe Vegas boots.

There was a bit of a kerfuffle behind me, but it didn't get close.

Sloan probably pushed it away with an invisible force field or something.

I chanced a glance at my soon-to-be tossed footwear.

"You loved those boots," Sloan said, with a certainty I wouldn't have expected from him in a gazillion light years.

I nodded, refusing to get choked up over something as silly as boots—even if they were more than simple footwear. I could count on them to bring out my confidence when I didn't feel it. They'd been one of my first large purchases when I got my first gig as a backup singer on an international tour.

And they'd been half off.

Sloan gave me a look like he got it. Understood and even commiserated.

Which meant... I had totally misread the situation. This guy had a girlfriend.

Because a guy didn't understand the loss of a pair of boots unless he either had the same affection for footwear—which I seriously doubted given the state of his boots—or he had someone in his life.

Yes, I'd done the obligatory check, and he wasn't wearing a ring, but that didn't mean anything. He hadn't touched my back at the party, and he'd been quiet most of the way down The Strip. Like he was trying to sort out a puzzle in his brain, and it gave him a headache.

"You're all partnered up. I knew it," I stated as a fact. "Damn. I was getting a tiny crush on you. What with the way you... are you?"

Whoever he was with was a lucky, lucky woman.

He stared at me funny for a long beat, the edges of his lips sort of twitching.

"My mom was into shoes." Sloan slung his arm around my shoulder. "She taught me the importance of designer."

I shivered. Too fucking good to be true.

"I don't do designer, but I respect the connection a person can have with shoes or handbags," he continued. "And I'm not partnered up."

Did he just say...?

"You're sure you don't have a significant other?" For clarity's sake and all.

Sloan shook his head, his arm still very much draped around me. I snuggled in and gave him a good sniff test.

Oh, he may have been all beard and boots, but he wore exceptional cologne. Something with undertones of sage and sea salt.

"I am single." He did the lip twitch thing again. "Tell me the part about the crush again?"

Ha. And hot damn.

Sloan scorched me with the heat in his gaze. My heart beat faster, and my mouth went dry.

This was the perfect one-night stand situation. He was, well, him. I was me. And we had limited bedroom space at the condo.

In fact, I'd be doing everyone a favor if I bunked up with Sloan.

"I said." I would've stepped further into his space to make a move, but without one heel, I worried I might tip right over. "I'm getting a tiny crush on you."

Not my best pickup line, but it'd have to do. Truly, I was out of practice. This was the problem when a girl was in a blah-de-dah relationship for too long. I'd totally lost my pickup game swagger.

"All right, then," he said, simply.

Seriously, that's all he said.

What the hell? I wasn't on a compliment fishing expedition, but would it have killed him to mention what that tube dress did for my chest? 'Cause it did a lot.

"I think I missed this whole thing." I gestured between us. "I thought you were into me."

Sometimes, the best thing a girl could do was to not beat around the bush, but to just throw it all out there.

"Maya, I like you." Sloan chewed on his cheek. "But I don't do messy." Sloan pushed his lips together. "I prefer things to be simple."

Well, then he should've avoided me. Though, in this case, there was nothing messy about any of it.

"Should we head back to the apartment for other shoes?" Sloan asked, and he had precisely the correct amount of sadness in his tone for the predicament. Surprise ex-husbands showing up out of the blue, ruined shoes, plus no martini equaled a pretty crummy night. Add to that, my stomach was gnawing on itself, asking for a buffet reprieve.

So, yes, I should go back home, raid the fridge, and swap shoes. That made the most sense.

Instead, I wanted to clarify something—

"This whole thing between us is super simple." I lifted my eyebrows on purpose.

There was no need for complications between the two of us.

Palate cleansers were for fun, not for deep conversations on the Vegas Strip.

"I'm single. I think you're wicked hot. And I like your flannel," I said, counting all the reasons this would work. "Also, your beard. I dig it. And I want nothing other than tonight with you. No offense or anything. I just think we could have fun with no expectations."

That bought me a grin.

"How's that for simple?" I asked.

"That's very... simple." Were his cheeks blushing red? I couldn't tell with the beard.

"Your turn." I tilted my ear to my shoulder.

"We have three options," he said, a sly grin tracing his mouth.

I didn't hate the way he licked at his lips as he spoke. Oh no, I didn't. Not at all. "I can't wait to hear them."

"One, you go shoeless." He glanced at my feet, a small flirtatious twinkle in his eye.

I wrinkled my nose. "Out here?"

"This is where we are." This, he said with a rough, gravelly tone I felt all the way in my panties.

The Strip wasn't exactly a sandy beach or even a brisk walk through a neighborhood. This was Las Vegas. Who knew what I might step on or in and what bacteria it might harbor.

"Two," he continued, still with that flirty glint. "We can go buy new shoes at a store around here." He lifted a shoulder and the simmering in his gaze?

My, my, my, I liked it.

"I'm game to watch you try on shoes," he finished, as though he were actually attempting to get me to try on shoes and take off every-freaking-thing else.

This option wasn't an unfortunate one. Actually, if done correctly, it could be very Cinderella... minus the whole stepsisters and dead parents. (My parents were very much alive.)

"What's option number three?" I asked.

"We go back to the condo. You change your shoes..." He trailed off like there was more to what he considered.

That was the rub of his three options. Changing my shoes was the most logical option. I had my back-up, second-choice sparkle booties that would work fine. Fine minus a solid dose of kitten-heel confidence.

"Or we both take off our shoes and stay in?" he finished, a slow grin spreading, which highlighted his beard nicely.

Oh. Hey there. There it was.

I'd even get to kiss him and... other stuff. I had never kissed a man with a beard before. Honestly, I hadn't realized it was a bucket list item until right there at that moment.

"I don't particularly want to drop a boatload on new shoes." I smiled what I hoped was a wicked grin with a heavy helping of coy.

"Then you should call your girls so they know you're staying in," he suggested. "They might get worried."

They wouldn't. This was Vegas. They'd be worried tomorrow if I didn't show, but I would text them the A-okay signal tonight, and they'd be good. Especially if I mentioned the broken boot and Sloan.

The two of us wouldn't get a lemon drop martini or buffet, but we could grab a sidewalk margarita and street tacos on the way back to the condo.

Margaritas paired excellently with one-night-stand bearded men.

This was such a perfect idea to break me back into the social scene of happiness and fun, and out of long-term romance and the relationships lugged along with it.

We found the most adorable margarita vendor. I whipped out my credit card, but Sloan made it there first with his Visa.

"Uh." I held up my card between two fingers. "You don't have to do that."

"It's already done."

Oh, well. That was hard to argue with.

I took a long pull of margarita and praised the heavens above for tequila and a hot guy date. Honestly, most days, I wondered who decided it was a good idea to let me be an adult. It took very little to make me happy.

Sloan's free hand pressed against my waist, and my body responded to that light touch like he'd just kissed the sensitive spot underneath my earlobe.

At that moment, I glanced at Sloan, oh-so-ready to make an entire night full of memories. Wonderful memories.

One-night-only memories that were totally inappropriate.

CHAPTER
FIVE

SLOAN

We'd finished our margaritas and after that, nothing seemed to matter anymore. Only Maya. Only the way my body wanted to be with hers. Inside hers. Only the way she welcomed me, and I wanted to be welcomed.

We didn't make it to the condo—the edges of how we'd stumbled into a swanky hotel lobby were fuzzy. But we couldn't keep our hands off each other, so we got a room.

Somehow—I wasn't entirely certain how it came about—we got the key card to work and made it inside the hotel room.

That's where we ended up in that moment, practically fused to one another. Hands on hips, lips on mouths, and moans coming from Maya that—

"I want your mouth between my legs," Maya said against my cheek as she rubbed her breasts against my chest.

Uh-huh, Maya's dirty talk was out of this world.

"I'm going to make you come on my tongue," I said against her lips, attempting to keep up with her.

We stumbled through to the living room; I couldn't say how,

but it happened. I held her against my body as she walked backward.

"What are you going to do next, Sloan?" she asked, her wide eyes and the desperation in her tone totally doing it for me.

"Maybe it's time we stopped talking about it, and I get to work?" I leaned in and kissed behind her ear, tracing my tongue down to her earlobe and kissing her there.

Fuck, she tasted good.

"Yes," she said, closing her eyes and tossing her head back. "Yes. Yes. All the yes."

"Bed?" I asked, my voice husky and rumbly. "Or shower?"

She opened her eyes long enough to say, "Definitely the bed."

We didn't actually make any forward progress toward the bed. No, because her arms wound around my neck, my mouth took hers again, and things moved faster right there beside the closed door, standing on the plush carpet of our suite.

Her breaths became more uneven as her eyes dilated from apparent desire. Still totally clothed, her body knew exactly what mine needed, and vice versa, what with the way she moaned my name as I slid my leg between hers, and she rubbed against me.

I wanted to move my fingers to pull off my shirt, but she was multi-tasking with the leg thing and unbuttoning me all at the same time.

I held her steady, even as I was more unsteady than I'd ever been. Everything was still mildly hazy around the edges.

I didn't mind because Maya tasted like tequila and lime and a great time.

I snort-laughed at my internal rhyme but managed not to stop kissing her. I should add ability to rhyme to my resumé, that's what I should do. Since my career was totally fucked, anyway, I'd make a new resumé, and I'd write it so it rhymed.

My manager would love that.

"What?" She pulled her mouth away from mine.

"Nothing." I held her jaw in my palm and went back to kissing her.

33

She leaned away, breathing heavy. "Seriously, why'd you laugh?"

"Because…" Okay, what the hell was I supposed to say? I ran my hand over my hair. "I…" I sighed. "I shouldn't be thinking about my resumé while you're unbuttoning me."

She stared at me as though she realized she'd been having this tryst with The King himself, and she wasn't sure what to do with that.

"You were thinking about your resumé?" She frowned as lines formed between her eyebrows. She crossed her arms.

I stepped toward her. "It was a funny thought. That's why I laughed, because there's only room in my head for you, and nothing else makes sense."

"That's remarkably sweet." She moved right back into unbuttoning my shirt. "I can see why that would be funny."

I walked her toward the bed. But it seemed like there might be two of them… I tried to refocus.

Shit.

My lack of momentum made her stumble slightly. I caught her.

Unfortunately, we both fell to the ground—her splayed on top of me.

I couldn't help it. I stuck my face in her neck and laughed. She laughed right along with me until our eyes met, and nothing seemed funny anymore. No, things felt like they had clicked into place for the first time.

Ever, ever.

Surely, she felt that, too. I couldn't be the only one.

Remember this…

Something deep down told me to hold onto the moment. A bone-deep something that I recognized as a gut feeling. One I shouldn't ignore.

Remember this…

She went into focus and then out again. I shook away the feeling.

"You think they put something in those drinks?" I asked. I didn't get quite this drunk off of one yardstick margarita.

"That'd be the tequila," fuzzy, double Maya said against my mouth.

Not that the woman had grown fur or become two people. They couldn't pour enough tequila to make that happen. Could they?

No. Clearly, no. Why would I even be thinking that? That made no sense. Time was being a funny asshole right now. Time felt fast and slow all at once, like someone had tried to fix the clock that was my life but was doing a shitty job of it, overcompensating each way.

The edges of life had a numb film that made me want to say, "screw responsibility" and go down on this woman.

Which was pretty much what I was ready to do right here, right now, with Maya and that fuzzy double Maya right beside her, who I knew in my brain wasn't real.

"How do we get to the bed?" she asked, pulling her bottom lip between her teeth.

"I don't know," I admitted. I didn't want to move, not with her right there covering me. Her dress hiked up to her ass, and her slip of a shirt pulled lower.

No, I didn't have a desire to get her to a bed. Instead of pushing myself up and getting us there, I traced my fingers over the back of her thighs, up to the curve of her ass. Holding her gaze with mine. Quirking an eyebrow in question.

Did you want this?

"Don't stop there," she said, squirming down until the center of her aligned with the tips of my fingers.

I smiled. Oh boy, did I smile, as I moved her thong underwear to the side and slid my finger along the seam between her legs.

She moaned, and I found the sweet bundle of nerves at the apex of her thighs, rubbing it with two fingers as her breaths became uneven, and she rubbed against the long length of my erection.

I should stand up, carry her to a bed, and finish things there.

Tonight, I wasn't very good at doing what I should do.

Remember this...

So instead of picking her up and taking her to the bed, I rolled, so she was on her back, and I was over the top of her.

Then I kissed my way along the edge of her body—over the fabric of her dress—and dipped my head between her legs to use my tongue as promised.

My fingers and tongue did their thing, while Maya's hands splayed in my hair, giving direction in her not-so-subtle way.

Oh yes, I would remember this.

As her release took hold, and her body convulsed around my fingers, I glanced up at her arched body to her face to watch as she came for me.

CHAPTER SIX

MAYA

What was that constant buzzing, and how could I make it stop?

My head pulsed with the kind of ache that only Las Vegas could induce. I knew that I should move, but there was something lovely about lying there in that warm bed with my eyes closed, wrapped up in those strong male arms.

Hold, up, where am I?

The buzzing stopped, and I peeled open one eye, then the other, revealing a room I had never seen before. The guy next to me? Him, I'd seen.

"Sloan?" I asked his name, quietly, testing to see if he was awake.

Other than his gentle up and down breaths, he didn't budge when I spoke his name.

I extracted myself from the arm draped over me and sat up, slowly, because that's the only way my body would move.

I was naked, and by the look of the hickey on my left breast and the lipstick imprints on Sloan's face, we'd had a very *nice* time.

I lifted the sheet and, yup, he was naked, too.

The long cords of his muscles were covered in a smattering of masculine dark hair that matched his beard. Let it be known that there was nothing manscaped about this man.

I liked it.

Even with the headache, the light pulse between my legs perked right up, so I set the sheet back down.

We'd stopped for margaritas, we drank them, and then... there was a giant blank spot in my memory.

I needed to check in with my friends—let them know I was good. Ensure they were also good.

The buzzing started again.

My phone, it was definitely my phone.

"Sloan." His name came out like a croak. I reached for his shoulder to wake him, and that's the precise second when my world tilted.

Because there was a giant-ass diamond ring on my left hand. I opened my mouth to shriek, but no sound came out. Pretty sure my heart was racing, and I'd started to sweat, but I was in the middle of an odd out-of-body experience so I felt none of that.

I couldn't say how long I stayed that way, stuck with my hand out and my mouth open.

"Hey." Sloan reached for my shoulder. Son-of-a-biscuit, he had a wedding band on his finger, too. "Maya?"

He didn't seem to notice his ring. Or mine.

"You okay?" He sat up much quicker than I did. Though he did wobble when he got to the top, and he blinked really hard. "Maya?"

I continued to stare at the diamond on my finger, unable to do anything other than just... look.

Sloan followed the path of my gaze. "Whoa."

Right, whoa?

I pulled the ring off and threw it. Straight up, hocked it across the room. It made a small *ti-i-nk* when it bounced off the television.

"That's better," I said, the words coming out all throaty.

Not quite, though. I reached for his hand, yanked off his ring, and threw it, too.

"Why was I wearing a ring?" he asked like it didn't really matter one way or the other.

The best thing about adrenaline was that it momentarily removed the hangover effects from before. I tossed back the sheet and stood.

I got slightly woozy but recovered. Even though I wasn't wearing a stitch of clothing, I scanned the room for any papers or envelopes. Anything that might give me a hint if we'd done this for real or just for fun.

"But it's never fun, is it?" I said, aloud.

"Maya, come back to bed," Sloan said, again like this was a normal occurrence for him.

I shuffled through the clothes tossed about the room. At some point last night, I'd acquired a new pair of boots. Dollars to donuts, I'd bet these hadn't been on sale. Somehow, I also came across my panties. Multi-tasking, I put them on while digging for my purse.

"Relax. Whatever's the matter, we'll deal with it." Sloan had a glazed, just-woke-up look.

His adrenaline clearly hadn't activated like mine.

"A-ha." I found a large manila envelope tossed on the sofa.

I knew this envelope. Because that's exactly how they handed out marriage licenses in Clark County. I looked to Sloan. He was oblivious and running his hand over his face like this wasn't the worst possible way to wake up.

I snagged the envelope in my grip, opened the seal, and my heart dropped because there was definitely a marriage license.

"No," I said. "No, no, no, no, no." Each no got progressively louder.

I sat on the sofa and stared at the license. There was another envelope marked with a Neon Nuptials Chapel logo, so I opened that one, too.

"Oh, God," I said, sifting through the photos.

39

Sloan and I with a Liberace actor in a chapel—clearly getting married. I dropped each photo to the floor as I went through them. The receipt in the middle said we'd splurged for the special package of memories.

Which was nice for us to have done, since I didn't remember a damn thing.

"Do you remember what happened?" I asked.

"No," he said. "I remember we got the margaritas. I was gonna call a ride share, but..." He reached to grab his phone, and he slid his thumb across the screen. "I didn't call a ride share." He blinked at his phone, rubbing his eyes.

My phone buzzed again.

I grabbed the nearest clothing—his flannel shirt. With my important bits covered, I checked my phone. I didn't answer Emily's call. Best not to let her know I broke the biggest rule of them all last night.

Instead, first, I confirmed they were good via their messaging. They were.

Then I shot out a quick:

> Emily & Angela: Hey, Gr8 Ngt. Everything's good here.

Then I figured I should add:

> Emily & Angela: Don't wry! I'm w/Sloan!

I checked my call history; I'd called no one last night. That was good. If I didn't call anyone, then they didn't know.

Except... I checked my social media accounts. Yep, nothing there, either.

"Did you call anyone last night? I didn't call anyone last night. And I didn't post anything on any socials. Did you? Did you post?" I asked quickly.

"Uh..." Sloth style, he checked his phone. "No. No calls, texts, or anything else." He paused to study a slip of paper next to his cell.

"Maya, where are the rings?" he asked, his gaze lingering on a slip of paper in his hands.

He tossed back the covers and slid his legs over the side of the bed, tagging his boxers and pulling them on.

"I don't know," I said, shaking my head.

"This was the direction you tossed 'em?" he asked, already getting down on his hands and knees to look through the thick carpet by the television.

"Why? Did we steal them?" I asked. "Oh, my God. We don't know. We probably five-finger discounted them." I pressed my hands in my hair, pulling it away from my face. "We're criminals. I'm going to prison."

"No, I have the receipt." He was still searching the carpet with his hands. "We didn't steal them, but they cost a fucking fortune." While he *was* searching for them, he wasn't super into it. Actually, he was being laidback about the whole thing.

"Do you have a hangover?" I asked. "Because I do."

"Yeah," he said, still searching. "My brain's on fire."

All things considered, he was handling the whole *woke up naked with a wedding band* shebang way too well.

Gah, I wasn't. The nauseating headache from whatever the bartender put in those tequila-infested yardstick cups was the absolute worst.

Bartender was a very loose sort of term for the man, because in hindsight, the guy was more of a hangover-inducing evil wizard. Extra emphasis on evil.

"Found one." Sloan slid my diamond band on his pinky and looked for the other.

"Sloan, I cannot be trusted as an adult," I said. "I am a grown-up human being, and I cannot be trusted." I bit my lips together, because soon, I'd start to cry and once that happened, everything would go to hell. The only thing worse would be to wake up married *and* pregnant. I wouldn't, because I was consistent with my birth control pills, but...

"Oh my God." Hangover notwithstanding, I practically leapt from the sofa. "Did we use protection? Tell me we used protection. Did you even bring condoms? Please tell me we practiced safe sex. I cannot get an STD! I *cannot*. My health insurance is total shit. It's the worst. You don't understand how bad it is. Like if there was a contest for the worst health insurance, my insurance would win that contest. I take extra vitamins every day, just because it's so crappy."

I checked the nearest trash can, but it was empty.

Damn.

"You didn't flush it, did you?" I asked. "Because if you flushed it, there will be no evidence. Also, it's really bad for the pipes and stuff to flush that kind of thing down."

"Maya," Sloan said, pausing his ring search. "Chill."

"I will not chill," I replied. "Now is not the time to chill."

I lifted the trash can nearest the bed to check it and—

"Oh, thank goodness. We were responsible." I held the trash can against my chest. Yes, all of the appropriate evidence suggested we may have been inebriated, but we were responsibly wasted.

"Found it," Sloan said, holding up the other ring and sliding it back on his finger.

Good thing I had the wastebasket on hand, because watching him slide that ring on his finger?

Any remnants left of that margarita came right up.

CHAPTER
SEVEN

MAYA

No matter what, accidentally finding myself married in Vegas, for the third freaking time, sucked.

I cleaned myself up. Sloan cleaned himself up. We both got some Ibuprofen and fluids on board, so the hangovers subsided a little. Then Sloan and I did what two people do when they wake up married and want to avoid reality a bit longer—we checked out of the hotel before going off to find breakfast.

While he settled up with the front desk, I checked in once more with Angela and Emily. I didn't mention my situation, and I sure as hell didn't offer to call. Nope, I just slipped my phone in my purse and pretended it didn't exist.

Then Sloan found us a restaurant, and I walk-of-shamed my way through the buffet line before plopping my ass down at a table to wait for him.

I added a pat of butter to my plate, smearing it to cover the entire top pancake before adding a touch of syrup. Then I pressed my fingertips against my temples to relieve the residual headache.

It didn't work because that wasn't a hangover cure.

Even more super sucky? If I knew myself, and I knew myself, those tears I dreaded were due to fall soon.

"Maya Mitchell, don't you cry," I said to myself as I blinked back a crap ton of wet. Not when it would only make the headache worse...and make my eyes puffy...and draw attention to me. I wanted zero of those things.

The plate in my new husband's hands landed on the table with a thunk that sounded like a thunderclap to my aching brain.

Of course, it didn't lightly clink. The plates at this buffet weren't glass; that would be entirely too good for two idiots who got drunk and got married. We deserved to eat our breakfast off of loud restaurant melamine.

Sloan sat across from me.

"Maya," he said my name like an apology. He shifted a bit in his chair. "It's... uh—"

"Where did you find French toast?" I asked—okay, it sounded like an accusation, and that wasn't at all what I meant. I closed my eyes, reset, opened them, and said, "I didn't see any when I went through."

His French toast looked way more appetizing than my pancakes.

He subtly pointed over my shoulder with his fork. My gaze slipped over to the buffet where, yep, I'd missed the French toast bar.

"Oh." I hiccuped. Still, I refused to all-out cry. I was a strong-ass, independent woman, dammit. "I didn't go that way."

Sloan opened his mouth like he was going to say something, then he cleared his throat and forked his toast. I understood he was likely cautious with words after the drama I'd tossed around when we'd woken up.

Betcha he seriously regretted his inebriated choices as well, given how he kept looking at me across the table like I was a bomb that might explode.

"Do you want some?" He totally offered me a bite of his French toast served up on the tines of his fork.

Time sort of stopped spinning in the right direction, and it felt like everything in the room paused. Everything but his fork lifted as an offering and his eyelids blinking over his brown eyes.

I may as well have been Alice falling into the rabbit hole of Wonderland with no control over anything.

And that was it.

That tossed me right over the edge into the land of tears.

One led the way down my cheek, and then another took off after.

Seriously, I tried to stop them, but between the tears, the hiccups, and the fact that I had pancakes when I really wanted French toast—it was basically a free-for-all dance party in my tear ducts.

"Hey." He set down his fork. And, dammit, he had the look of a guy who was going to do something sweet and try to comfort me. Which, for the record, would make things that much worse. With some flannel-wrapped comfort, the tears would really roll.

"I just…need…a…" I did my very best to rein in my emotions. "… second." I waved him away while I shoved all those heavy feelings deep, deep down.

There. Much better.

"You're handling this so much better than me." For a first-timer, this whole sitch was entirely too easy for him.

"I have an idea," he said, and, honestly, I didn't totally dig the way he said that because some kind of echo in my memory flitted through. A memory where he said that same thing, and then his mouth was on my navel, his teeth scraping along my belly button, down to—

I squirmed in my chair. I did. It happened.

The nerves along my abdomen purred at an inappropriate-for-breakfast memory.

"Let's just figure out what comes next." He lifted a forkful of eggs to his mouth. "That always makes me feel better when shit goes sideways."

Eating eggs was the least sexy food a person could eat. No

matter what, eggs weren't an attractive food. And yet... I didn't mind Sloan and his eggs.

They weren't sexy, for sure. But they did nothing to diminish his hotness quotient at all—something truly surprising and definitely worth noting.

"You ready to sort everything?" he asked, oblivious to the amount of hot guy energy he tossed around just sitting there eating.

"Everything?" I heard myself ask, pulling myself out of the watching-him-eat trance. Surely, he couldn't mean everything.

Somewhere deep in the dregs of my memory, an image of his tongue traced along the back of my knee. Little goosebumps trailed there, up, up, up—

"Yeah." He shrugged.

I shook off whatever that was in my brain. I couldn't think about getting turned on by my husband. A totally off-limits husband because if we did it again, it would complicate the entire situation.

Ask me how I know?

"There's a lot of everything we'll have to go through to get out of this mess," I said. "So much of everything that all of the every-things are totally overwhelming."

His lips twitched, and he looked like he wasn't sure what to do with me. Nothing new, I got that a lot.

Though he recognized my lack of humor, because he locked down any residual lip twitching.

"Let's start with the simple everything," he suggested, continuing to eat his breakfast like it was no big deal, and he wasn't a hot football player in flannel, eating eggs with his accidental bride. "What's the first thing on your mind?"

Other than the tongue thing? Or the sexy eating?

"We got married," I said, figuring I should just keep practicing the words so when I had to say them again, they wouldn't sound so funky.

"We did." He nodded. "Seemed like a good time. What do we

do after breakfast?" he asked, carefully, like this conversation had entered minefield territory.

"I'll have to call Warren, so he'll meet us at the courthouse on Monday morning."

"Warren?"

"My favorite Clark County clerk."

Sloan set his fork aside and folded his hands under his chin. "You have a favorite clerk here?"

His phone rang. He glanced at the screen, his expression unreadable. Then he tapped out a message.

"Sorry. Work stuff." He met my gaze across the table.

Then his phone rang again. He glanced at the screen again. Tapped out something else. Then more.

This appeared as if it might take a bit, so I blew out a breath and practically inhaled my pancakes. Then I arranged the slices of bacon so they were ready after my dose of carbs.

"You look like you're thinking really hard over there," he said, done with his phone stuff.

But his phone chimed again. He glanced at it… again. And he frowned at it… again. Then some kind of dawning brightened his eyes.

I couldn't quite vocalize it, but I was pretty sure I wouldn't like what came next.

CHAPTER EIGHT

SLOAN

Elliott and my management team were already at work that morning in one of their let's-fix-Sloan's-problem meetings, which meant Elliott was bombarding me with ideas. He didn't want my opinion. But if he looped me in, then I couldn't claim I didn't know. This was all part of how he worked.

But I had bigger issues to sort, and he had to wait.

A lock of hair fell loose around Maya's forehead. I forced myself not to reach out and push it back. She may have been my wife for the moment, but I didn't have the permission to do that.

Instead, I focused on her amber eyes and not the Elvis looka-like grabbing coffee or the Dolly lookalike filling a plate of pancakes.

"Someday," she said, pursing her lips. "God, as my witness, I'll have a wedding that I get to plan, a wedding night I get to enjoy, with a husband who will last longer than two weeks. Do you even know how pissed my mom is going to be that she missed another Maya wedding? So pissed. There's no getting out of it." She took a deep breath and continued, "You've got to quit doing this to us." She mimicked what had to be her mom's voice. "Like they're the ones suffering." She pointed at me with her fork. "They aren't. They probably don't even have a headache."

"At least you don't have to deal with Elliott," I said, trying to lighten the moment. "He's gonna lose his mind when I tell him about this." Which was why I didn't plan to do it soon.

"Take my advice. Wait until the hangover goes away before you bring it up," she suggested.

"You know a lot about this," I said, as some of her comments from the night before slithered back into my brain.

"Look, a girl doesn't get married multiple times in Sin City without figuring a few things out," she said.

"Exactly how many times have you been married?" I asked.

"Not a lot." She dabbed the edge of her lips with her napkin.

"Maya?"

"You know about Dan. It's not a secret that this isn't my first time."

"Okay. But how many—"

She didn't wait for me to finish the question. "Total of three. Two others, plus you." She lifted her palms in apparent defense. "One divorce. One annulment. One…" She gestured between us. "In process."

"Okay." Now, I frowned.

"You might have just given me my least favorite response of all the responses," she said, matching my frown.

"I don't… Huh," I said.

"I know. Me either," she said. "And I've got a season pass on this ride."

"My management team has been kicking around ideas for… how'd they put it?" How did I word this? "'Diverting the spotlight off my loss of endorsement deals and my lack of reliability.'"

"I guess that makes sense," she said halfheartedly, with a small shrug.

"Does it?" I asked. She may have only been my temporary wife, but I hoped she'd be more on my side here.

"I mean, you've switched pro teams a few times, right?" she asked.

The question was innocent, but it still stung. Yeah, sure, Denver was the first place I'd stuck, and I was now playing for a contract extension. Also, Elliott had to issue corrections more often than he'd like because I said something stupid... there was also that.

"Just because it took time to find the right team doesn't mean I'm not reliable," I countered.

"Okay," she said, just like I had before.

I frowned. "That might be *my* least favorite response of all the responses."

"We'll blame it on the booze," she said with a smile.

Huh, the thing was, intoxicated us might've been onto something other than a one-night stand last night.

"Do you think people love a good love story?" I picked at my French toast with the tines of my fork.

She thought about my question. "Sure, I guess."

"Why?" I asked.

Her eyebrows fell together as she said, "Because everybody wants to hope for the best in people, and the idea of picking one person out of the entire world to be your human match? Well, I guess that's the true story of possibility."

A story of reliability, perhaps?

"I just had an idea," I said, carefully feeling out the idea in my head. "It's kind of unorthodox." To put it mildly.

"What's the idea?" Maya asked, some color back in her cheeks now that she dove into her breakfast.

"Well, we're married."

"Not for long," she said, pulling her lips in a thin line.

"What if we stayed married?" There I said it.

Maya stared, blinking at me with the type of horror like I'd accidentally scored a winning touchdown for the other team in overtime during post-season.

I shifted uncomfortably in my seat.

She crossed her arms and tossed me a serious look that sort of turned me on.

I should've gone back to eating my eggs, but I wasn't hungry anymore. Not when the fluorescent lights of the buffet flickered over my future.

"So this"—*Don't say mistake*—"thing we did could actually be beneficial. Long term," I said.

She stopped the blinking and stared with a glazed look that made me rethink my word choices and all thoughts about how this might work.

"As a bonus, I actually like you. That's a trait you want in a husband."

Maya's terror was now past a crushed car and well into house-sized square footage.

I should say something else and take back the words.

That didn't happen because I didn't want to take them back. Yeah, being married was a little extreme. So what?

There were loads of other reasons, too. More logical reasons.

"My reliability factor would go way up. And it could help you, too, right?" I asked. "I mean, there's gotta be something out of this for you."

"You." Maya pointed to me, her words dazed. "Really want to stay married to me?" She pointed at herself.

"Yes." I nodded.

More of the glazed staring came from her side of the table, this time with a small tilt of the head.

I set my fork aside, since there was no chance I'd be eating any more breakfast soon.

I wanted to know her. That was the first thought I'd had when I walked through the door of the condo, and Elvis took a dive into Maya's cleavage and tried to push down her top.

Of course, I remembered *that*.

I remembered the party, and Dan, and the shoe situation outside the M&M Store. Remembered a few pulls of my margarita.

After that, there was a whole blank section. I didn't remember a thing about what went down after we drank those margaritas.

Small tastes came back at odd times: little breaths of a memory. Personally, I'd never done the long-term thing—never made it that far along.

"The problem with a normal relationship is that there are too many expectations," I said, leaning into the conversation. "I mean, I've got other priorities and don't have time to do this for real. But here we are, and we could do it like this. You want a solo career? I've got some connections to help with that."

Last night's drunk me bought Maya a ring, and that was more than half a marriage right there.

"What we have between us isn't love at first sight or love at all." Maya tapped her fingertips on the table. "It's not a love story."

"Of course it isn't," I agreed. "Not a real one, anyway. That's what makes it perfect. Neither of us is coming into this with expectations. We stay married. I play football. You do whatever you want to do."

"I was wrong." Maya sat back in her chair, but now, she blinked again, and the glazed look was gone.

"What were you wrong about?" I asked, cautiously, moving into the situation with the same caution I'd take when approaching a new playbook.

"I thought this headache was the worst part of the morning. It isn't." Maya rubbed at her temples.

"What's the worst part?" I asked.

"That you're actually suggesting we stay married." She gestured to me. "You're sitting there with your brown eyes, and that beard that I don't even get to remember playing with, telling me you want to stay married when we absolutely cannot do that. And we used up all of our one-night-stand time totally inebriated. So, even if I was entertaining the idea of staying married—which I'm not—I don't even know if we're good together in… that way. That's an important thing to know, you know?"

"We were good together," I said confidently. I remembered

little, only a few minor details. Details I really liked... "I don't have to remember it to know we were good together." A memory of Maya's lips around my—

"There's no way to know." She threw her hands in the air. "And we can't do it again."

Hold up. Exactly why couldn't we—

"Here's the thing. Let me illustrate." She set out the salt and the pepper on the table between us. Nudging them close together. "Do you want to be Salt or Pepper?"

I didn't really care but decided on the fly, "Pepper."

"I sort of thought I'd be Pepper." Maya frowned, thought entirely too hard about it before saying, "Whatever, I can be Salt."

I'd never been in this situation before, but I figured it'd be best to keep my trap shut.

"This is Salt." She held up the salt shaker. "She has been avoiding all things Las Vegas for years because the last time she was here, she made some bad choices. She's finally ready to get back to her favorite town when she meets Pepper." She walked the pepper shaker over to Salt. "They have fun together. Drink too much. And then Pepper proposes to Salt." She did a puppet show, with Pepper pretending to nudge up against Salt.

Salt acted as surprised as an inanimate object could act.

"They're both compromised because of drinks. So, they get married," Maya said.

I didn't know where she was going with this puppet show, but there was one point I needed to correct.

"Hold on." I reached for the shakers. "Can I try?"

She let me take the props. "By all means."

"Pepper is minding his own business, playing football, when he makes an offhand comment about the sugar content of electrolyte drinks in front of a reporter. That one comment pisses off lots of people, so he has to get out of town. His buddies tell him they're all going to Vegas." I set down Pepper and lifted a jam packet and butter packet, walking them toward the minding-his-own-business Pepper. "'If you're gonna leave town, make it someplace fun.'" I did a shit job mimicking Finn and Elliott. "So, Pepper agrees to a Vegas weekend to get Butter and Jam off his ass." That didn't quite sound the way I'd hoped. "Pepper meets a pretty woman named Salt." I pushed the jam and butter away, moving the pepper shaker to Salt. "They drink margaritas, and Pepper pleases Salt and gives her a mind-blowing time in the bedroom because that's what Pepper does." I gave her a look I hoped punctuated that point. "Then Salt asks Pepper to marry her." I pushed the shakers back to Maya. "You can continue now."

"Salt would never do that."

"But Salt *did* do that."

"Pepper and Salt both said they remember nothing about the night before, so how does Pepper know if he or Salt did the asking?" Maya's chest was turning pink as she spoke, splotches of red dotting along her neck to her fair-skinned collarbone.

The last thing I wanted to do was go backward in our negotiations when we hadn't even moved forward.

"You don't have any bits of memory that are coming back? But when you showed me the wedding photos this morning, I distinctly remembered your suggestion that we get married."

"That's impossible because it didn't happen."

"We were in bed. We were naked. We were both drunk as snot from the tequila. I sounded like I was talking in cursive, and you took a header into the pillow when you tried to sit up."

"Oh." She scrunched her face up. "Then I talked about how bad I want a solo career. Then—"

"You suggested we get married. Look at us, remembering." I used Pepper to do a high-five with Salt.

"But we don't even know if we're compatible because we know next to nothing about each other. So, it makes sense that we move on with our lives. I know, from experience, that if you don't get an annulment quickly, it can be an entire problem with the legal system." Maya held Salt and pretended she spoke to Pepper. "Act on the annulment train fast, or it can get complex." She continued miming a conversation. "Sometimes, you have to go the divorce route. No one wants to go the divorce route. There's tons more paperwork with that option."

I reached for Pepper. "May I?"

She nodded. "Yes."

"It's a good thing I married you, Salt, because you're a marriage expert." I continued to talk through my Pepper puppet.

The edge of Maya's knuckle pressed lightly against mine. Nothing other than platonic, but we may as well have been standing at the altar.

She'd touched me with her knuckle then. All smiles as Liberace read the vows.

I'd been happy as all fuck when she lifted her knuckles and ran them along the edge of my beard.

My phone buzzed near my hand on the table. I ignored it. Honestly, her headache was rubbing off on me, what with trying to keep up with the puppet show.

We sat there on opposite sides of the table with Salt and Pepper and a lot of awkward settling right there on the table between us.

"The thing is, I used to be in love with the idea of being in love. But I don't feel that way anymore. This is *not* a love story." Her eyes pleaded with me to understand. The thing was, I understood. I understood perfectly.

I pulled myself taller and said, "All of this? It's exactly why this marriage will work."

CHAPTER NINE

MAYA

"The marriage will work," he said, as though I didn't hear him the first time.

For real though, why did he keep saying that?

I shook my head. "There's no way it will work. Here's the plan. Monday morning, you and I head to the courthouse." I held firm to that stance. "We do our thing there—sign the dotted lines and file the papers. Then we go our separate ways. Nobody even knows what happened this weekend." Honestly, not even the two of us. "Let's keep it that way."

Sloan grimaced.

I didn't like that grimace.

Then he pulled his lips to the side. Unfortunately, that look did nothing to thwart his curb appeal. Was it too much to ask that he not be good looking while we discussed ending our marriage?

"Here's what I'm thinking instead." He pushed his plate to the side and leaned in so he didn't have to speak so loudly.

Given how this entire conversation had gone so far, I was fairly confident that I wouldn't want to hear whatever he was about to say.

So, I also pushed my plate to the side. Leaned in and said, "I already don't like what you're thinking."

"If it's the assets part of this, and you're worried, I'm not out to get your stuff. I can have a lawyer draw up a post-nuptial agreement, so you're protected," he suggested. "I don't mind doing that. It makes sense."

"You mean so you're protected? I mean, it's not like backup singers make the same cake as pro-football players." Not even in the realm of the same number of commas and zeros on the checks.

He held up his hands like he was saying *wait a second*, but with his hands instead of words.

"I don't know what your financial situation is," he said. Dammit, he was genuine. "But I want to be clear that I respect that what's yours is yours. I, just, I want you to think about becoming comfortable with my idea. Don't discount it without giving it a shot."

I did one of my few parlor tricks and lifted my left eyebrow. I didn't have many of those, but I could roll my tongue over both ways and roll my eyes so only the white showed.

I paused for five seconds, counting each of them out in my head.

"Okay, I've thought about it. We should annul," I said.

Actually, then he rolled his eyes in what was clearly a mock defeat. Mock because there was no way a guy like Sloan admitted defeat easily.

His eye roll wasn't a full all-white version like I could pull off —there was still pupil.

His phone chimed with an incoming text. This time, he glanced at the screen. "I need to—"

He held up the phone.

"You should take it," I said. Whoever was on the other line could talk some sense into him, and then we could continue on with our annulment plans.

"Hey, Elliott," he said into the phone, then paused. Frowned.

"No. How did you..." He paled. The way the color drained from his hairline to his beard line was really sort of impressive.

If it hadn't meant he was one hundred percent freaking out.

"Are you okay?" I asked. That shade of white couldn't be healthy.

"They know," he said in a way that made my headache brew into a full migraine. "All of them. Everyone. They know about us."

"Who are all of them?" Like *all of them,* all of them, or just our close friends group, all of them? And what, precisely, did they know?

"The entire world," he said, putting his finger over the microphone on the phone. "They know we got married."

I blinked away the surprise.

"No," he said into the phone. "That's not..." He glanced at me with wild eyes. "No. I know how it might look."

Mad points for keeping his tone light as he spoke when he was clearly freaking the hell out.

Personally, I was in that odd calm before the storm. Like I knew the wind was about to blow me over, but right then, everything was A-okay, so I went with it.

But Sloan? Sloan was sweating.

Bet he wished right about then that he'd gone with a choice other than flannel.

"There's no way anyone can know," I whispered. Was I assuring him or me, or maybe us both? But there was no way for anyone to know what happened.

Tone still light, he clearly tried to keep his demeanor upbeat. But the frown lines around the edges of his eyes deepened.

That wasn't good.

I toyed with the edge of my coffee cup, giving a sidelong glance to the salt and pepper shakers and how simple life was three minutes ago when we'd been arguing with them.

Cell still pressed to his ear, Sloan hadn't said another word, blinking at his now-cold eggs, avoiding eye contact with me, and giving the occasional grunt in response to whatever Elliott said on the other end of the line.

"No," he said into the receiver as he shook his head. "That won't work. Nope. You're misunderstanding the whole thing."

My phone dinged. I didn't want to do it, but I glanced at the screen.

Angela: smthn 2 tell?

Angela was my best friend, and we told each other everything.

But if she already knew, what did it matter if I confirmed it right away or later? Of course, I would tell her once we got it all dealt with. The thing is that when we made it so nothing had happened, there would be nothing to tell.

"Social media," he said under his breath, pointing at my cell. "Check your socials."

Time around me seemed to freeze.

Angela texted a browser link at that exact moment.

I clicked on it because, clearly, I was a masochist.

As soon as I clicked, I wished I hadn't. Hoo boy, did I wish I hadn't.

Because there on the Instagram page of the Vegas wedding chapel was a collage of our photos from the night before. A collage of our wedding with confetti graphics and a big congratulations sticker as a banner over the top of the online gallery.

My heart nearly stopped. The knowledge that I was toast smacked me right upside the head. Figuratively, that is, since I only had pancakes on my plate.

Now, it was my turn to sweat, and I wasn't even wearing a flannel.

A vision of Sloan straddling me on the bed slid right into my consciousness. That feeling of him inside me made my heart race and my core tingle.

Ack, I couldn't think about that. Not right now. This was crisis time, not the time for my brain to throw around steamy memories.

I focused on the post. A post that included congratulations and our full names. Oh, look… someone had tagged our accounts and the Denver Stallions football account.

Dear God, there were hashtags.

And this was Sloan Stevens, so people knew who he was.

I clicked over to my account and sucked in a huge breath. Huh, this was weird.

My follower count had more than quadrupled, and the numbers were going up by the second. The little singing-in-the-living-room videos I made for fun were spreading. The one from last night had reached first-level viral territory.

Bonus, social media land was actually being nice.

Who is this person and why doesn't she have a record deal?

Where's she been hiding?

Next year, she'll be singing at the Mega Bowl.

This could be… could it be? I mean, this could be that big break I'd been waiting on.

I glanced at Sloan.

Could I do this? Gah, no, I couldn't pimp myself out for a coupon code to fame. That was wrong.

Then again, the damage was done, and we could let this thing roll.

My longest marriage was to Dan, and it had lasted barely over two weeks before he served me with papers. Maybe if I broke that record, I could call it a win?

Grr, that wasn't how things worked.

Unless it was how they worked.

Carefully, Sloan clicked off his phone and set it down like it was made of dynamite. Then he lifted his gaze to me and time started up again. In a good way that I wouldn't think about at all.

"What if—" I had a great thought I was ready to pounce on. "You and I stay married."

The way his eyes widened with simple shock was worth the price of admission. "Huh?"

I nodded along with my thought process now that I'd climbed on board his crazy train. "Let's let it happen for a bit. After a few weeks of pretend relationship time, our breakup can devastate you. In the meantime, my social media presence will grow, and maybe I'll get that big break. I'll finally be on the map. Nobody loses."

He shook his head, adamant. "Two weeks isn't long enough to prove my reliability or get you solidly pinned on that map. Why put a deadline on it? I mean, I think this could work for us. Long term."

Was he for real? A person didn't accidentally get married to a pro football player in Vegas and then stay married. Did they?

"Just think about it?" he asked. "No deadlines, just us making it work."

Perhaps Sloan was right and having him as my perpetual plus-one might save me a bunch of headaches. Future headaches because the current one was a hell of a doozy.

"If we're going to do this, then communication is absolutely key. We have to treat this as a partnership and say what needs to be said. Not worry if it might sound bad or hurt feelings. Don't you think?" I asked. "We just get it out there so we can deal with it. Whatever 'it' is."

"Agreed." He flashed a wide smile that I'd do nearly anything to see again. "The problem with every relationship I've ever been in has been that women don't straight-up say what they want from me. I have to guess, and I'm not a good guesser."

"Okay, so, first, that's incredibly sexist to group all women together like that. And second, you're in luck because I have no problem telling you what I want and what to do. I'm extremely efficient like that."

"Apologies for the comment I made that came across as sexist," he said. "I should've clarified my statement to 'all my former relationships.' Though they were all with women, that isn't a point that matters."

"See? Look at that. We can totally do this. You screw up, you apologize. You clarify. I think that this could be rule number one in our marriage."

"Does it go both ways?" he asked with those damn puppy eyes of his. "You also apologize and clarify?"

"For sure." As if I'd need to.

"Everything will be under control," he said. "It's the perfect marriage, if you ask me."

"One thing, though," I added, holding up my one-more-thing fingertip.

"Hit me." He gave me the go-ahead gesture.

"I think we should be married, married," I said, raising both eyebrows in hopes he understood.

"Agreed," he said with a quick nod. "Married, married."

"What I mean is I enjoy sex," I added.

"I also enjoy sex," he confirmed.

"Maybe we need to be sure we're compatible that way?" I asked, because it'd really be a drag if we weren't bedroom compatible, but we were stuck with each other.

As if my brain had it all queued up and ready to roll, a memory of the feel of him moving inside me and my legs wrapped around his back played through my thoughts.

"We're compatible that way," he said with confidence, as though he'd had the same memory at the same time.

"Great, I want to have sex. I think we should have sex." I grabbed my water glass and took a gulp.

"I love sex. Sex is great," he agreed. "Love it."

I choked a bit on the water because I should clarify that I meant sex with each other.

Not that I didn't understand why open marriages worked for some couples. I just... I didn't like to share. Never had.

"But only with each other?" I confirmed. "I mean, I think we should keep it to us, don't you? I don't want to hear that you've been playing the field while you're away playing the game."

"Maya, I don't want variety. I've never wanted variety. I just... I hate the unspoken expectations that I'm supposed to guess at," he said. "I don't like to guess."

"Then no guessing here." None.

"Does it go both ways?" he asked the same question from moments before. "We both stay inside the marriage? I don't really love the idea of you being on tour and—"

"For sure," I answered, the same way he had before.

"I have to live near Denver. For the team," he said. "Is that a problem for you?"

I shook my head. "I have a small apartment in Los Angeles, but I travel a lot when there's a tour, so it doesn't really matter where I'm based."

"We'll both be traveling a lot," he said.

"That's probably what will make it work even better," I said with a laugh. "The best part is that I think I could really like you, Sloan."

"I could really like you, too, Maya."

"And there's no risk of falling in love," I added.

"None." He nodded along. "We're not falling in love."

"Because that's what complicates everything," I agreed.

"And if there's something we want to know from each other, then we ask. Something we need to have from each other, we ask, yeah?" he said.

Sloan studied me as I studied him.

"And if we need to re-open any of our foundational rules, then we just have another salt and pepper talk," I suggested.

He smiled in agreement.

"There won't be any misunderstandings," he said. "Because we already know the rules."

"No expectations, because they've already been laid out," I said.

"Agreed, Mr. Stevens. Let's do this." I put my hand out to shake his, but he didn't shake it.

Oh no, he took my hand and lifted my knuckles to his lips, pressing a kiss there.

I shivered, which was silly because my whole inside somehow became warm at only that kiss.

"Deal," he confirmed.

CHAPTER
TEN

MAYA

I was doing this.

We were doing this.

I even put the ring back on and didn't even consider losing my breakfast over it.

The full implication of my actions hadn't quite hit me until right in that moment as Sloan and I left our breakfast table, exited onto The Strip, and headed into the real world where everyone knew our business.

Both of my sisters texted me. I ignored those.

Angela's texts couldn't continue to be ignored, however.

> Angela: Come bk. We need 2 tlk

> Maya:

> Angela: Don't   @ me. E is pissy

Because I went around her 'don't get married' rule? That was fair.

Maya: R U Pissed?

This was the third time Angela hadn't gotten to play maid of honor.

Angela: No! But I need deets. A football player rly?

I glanced at the man in question. The man was so very different from any other I'd ever married (or even dated). He was texting on his phone as we walked, glancing up here and there so he didn't plow into anyone.

Emily: hv u lost ur mind?

Maya: that's likely.

Emily: Annulment Monday?

Maya: …

I took a deep breath and didn't respond.

My phone rang, because of course it did. Emily would want to handle this verbally.

I glanced at the screen on my cell.

Then my heart skipped—and not in the good way Sloan had made it skip last night in front of the M&M Store.

This wasn't Emily. This was my mother.

I should answer it. I knew this, even willed my thumb to slide over the screen to take the call. Unfortunately, no matter what my mind said, my body wasn't into it.

Uh-huh, because my mother would kill me.

Emily: U kno I luv u. I'm worried.

Aw, that was sweet.

Maya: Headed bk 2 condo. Catch u in a sec.

I gripped the phone, and, with every ounce of myself, I willed my thumb to slide across the screen and answer Mom's call.

Aha! It worked.

"Mom," I said, holding the phone to my ear and forcing my voice to spill over with perky wedded-bliss happiness. "You won't believe it. I have news." I kept my voice as cheerful as possible, but it sounded fake. I knew it sounded fake.

Sloan turned us toward the fence in front of the Bellagio fountains. I didn't even stumble—not once!—as he pulled me to the side of the walkway, tucking me beside him so everyone else gave us space.

Was it odd that I caught a whiff of his scent and leaned in for more?

No, not odd. We were married. I could sniff him really good. Which wasn't bad because, gah, he smelled so... Sloan.

This wasn't his cologne from the night before. This scent was one-hundred-percent male and flannel. Yes, that was a scent combination. Oh boy, did it work.

"Maya," Mom said my name like a greeting. Like she didn't already know what had happened. But I wasn't a dunce, and I understood how the information tree shook all the gossip leaves over the many branches of my family.

"You have news?" Mom asked, with a note of steel that didn't bode well for me.

"Mom." I glanced up at Sloan, his brown eyes staring down at me and fortifying my defenses. That was nice. Lots of support emanated from him. "I got married. Again."

"Uh-huh," Mom said. "Your sisters both sent me the Instagram links. Which is why I called to tell you I'm not speaking to you." Mom let that sink in. "I just wanted you to know."

Well, fudge.

I thought over all the things I could say:

Don't worry. It's all under control.

You're gonna like him!

He didn't panic at all.

I really think he's a great guy.

Of those options, I said none of them. I opened my mouth and said—

"You're gonna love Sloan." *Say something else. Keep going, Maya.*

Sloan's eyebrows raised, and his eyes got sort of melty. Then the edges crinkled along with his smile.

"We're going to stay married." I cleared my throat. Why was everything so damn dry in the desert?

"You meant to marry this one?" Mom asked, carefully. Her mom-bullshit radar was clearly activated and ready to diagnose any disinformation I relayed.

"Yes," I said. This was no lie because the Maya of last night had clearly meant to marry him. "It was a surprise to both of us. But we did it. And we've spent the morning talking. Making plans. We did things differently than I have before."

All true.

Somehow, and I wasn't entirely certain how it had happened, my hand slid into Sloan's. Did he reach for me, or did I reach for him? I didn't know. Couldn't say. That didn't matter, though, because Sloan had my back.

"Mom." I glanced at a piece of chewed-up gum that hundreds of steps from loads of people had worn into the concrete sidewalk. "I think you're going to like Sloan."

He squeezed my hand at that, like he was making a promise… or he was telling me to stop talking?

But when I said that Mom would like him, it was the truth. He was an extremely likeable guy.

"Is he there?" Mom asked. "With you?"

Um… "He's here. Yes."

"I want to talk to him," Mom said.

Eh… "I don't think that's a great idea."

"Hand him the phone," Mom insisted.

The way my mom said this with just the right amount of kindness and a solid dose of no-nonsense had me handing the phone to Sloan.

"Sloan," he said, holding my cell to his ear.

Drat, I should've put it on speakerphone first.

"Mmm-hmm," he said, nodding along. "Yes, ma'am." He frowned. "No, ma'am." Then the edges of his lips twitched with humor. "Of course, ma'am." He grinned a flash of white. "Looking forward to it."

He handed the phone back. I said my goodbyes and tucked the cell in my pocket.

"What did she say?" I asked as he maneuvered us back into the stream of people walking the same direction.

He glanced at me, his eyes warm like they wrapped me in a blanket. "I'm not at liberty to discuss that."

"Sloan."

"Maya."

I let out a long breath, knowing arguing wouldn't get me anywhere.

"Your mom is worried about you," he said, pulling his lips between his teeth. "She told me you aren't always as strong as you want people to think."

"Is anyone?" I asked, taking in the artificial lake outside the ritzy hotel.

"See that?" He dropped my hand and pointed in that direction.

"The lake?" I confirmed, in case he'd spotted the Tarzan guy again, and there would be a mosh pit coming our way.

He nodded. "During the day like this, it's clear it doesn't belong here. It's too blue. Too perfect. But at night? When the lights come on and the city comes to life, it shines. Same thing with a football stadium, you know?"

"I really don't." Football wasn't my jam, but that was a discussion for later.

"During the practices, it's just a field. But when the fans show up, and we rush the field right before a game? It's electric."

"The stage is the same," I agreed. "Before a performance, it's just wood and metal and speakers, but once everything comes together, it works, you know?"

He nodded. "Exactly."

"You think that's how we are? We're like the field or the lake or the stage?"

"Yeah."

"So, us together. Are we on the field before the game or after it starts?" I asked.

Were we Las Vegas during the day when the shine dulls and the grunge factor rises to a solid ten? Or Las Vegas at night when it's magical?

"I guess that's what we're about to find out," he said.

I knocked on his shoulder lightly, jokingly, with my fist.

Instead of bouncing off, it stayed there. Like my hand didn't want to move, even though I was telling it to with my brain.

Sloan reached for it, and something changed in the air. Something happened. One of those things I had no control over.

Not when I stepped forward into his space, and he pulled my hand to his lips. Kissing the underside of my wrist and turning me right the hell on.

He moved into my space, and I didn't even care that he was there. His lips brushed mine. Just a touch. Nothing invasive or too much. Just something that edged a memory I actually wanted to remember.

"We're definitely Las Vegas at night," I said. We had to be, with that kind of a sizzle from a brush of a kiss.

He chuckled and nodded. "Agreed."

CHAPTER ELEVEN

SLOAN

This wasn't going well.

We'd made it back to the condo, but as soon as we announced our "we eloped" reveal, it didn't feel like an apartment anymore. It felt like we'd walked into one of those giant *thwap* mousetraps, and the bar clamped down on us.

Elliott stood next to the Elvis bust that had accosted Maya yesterday.

Maya reached for my hand, and I couldn't tell whether it was for my benefit or hers.

Elliott shook his head as though he were a disgruntled parent instead of an agent who took home fifteen percent of my earnings. "This continuing cascade of questionable decisions has to stop."

I'd bet he'd prepared that line ages ago and had been saving it for the right scenario. Because he didn't even stumble over the words—and there were a lot of words.

'A cascade of questionable decisions' was a pre-planned word salad if I'd ever heard one.

"An annulment is the best choice here," Emily added, standing beside Elliott and crossing her arms just like his. "Hands down, the best choice."

"I mean, this has to rate up there with your most questionable antics of all time," Elliott continued.

"Wait." Angela turned to Elliott. "Why is marrying Maya questionable? Maya's great. He's lucky to get to marry Maya."

Elliott pursed his lips and stared at the floor. "It's not about Maya. We're trying to avoid more scandal here—not come up with new creative ones. A quickie marriage and then an annulment doesn't look good for him."

"But at least he didn't talk more shit about ZipZing," Finn said, but no one was paying any attention to him.

"Let's all be sure to worry about what's important here: Sloan's reputation." Emily tossed her arms wide and nearly clocked her brother.

He ducked in time.

"Hey, everyone," Maya said, loud enough to get everyone's attention. "It's all good. We're going to stay married."

"There's no annulment. No divorce." I stared straight at Elliott. "No scandal."

Emily, Angela, Elliott, and Finn said nothing for entirely too long. They all just blinked in near unison.

Finn laughed like we'd told an exceptionally funny joke. No one else laughed. The defensive stronghold of Maya's girlfriends... and Elliott...didn't find this amusing.

"So, you planned this whole thing and didn't think to loop me in?" Elliott asked.

"No, we didn't plan it," I corrected.

"I mean, if we'd planned it, don't you think we'd have invited you all?" Maya asked, her fingers still tangled with mine. "We don't even remember getting married."

"But that doesn't mean we're getting an annulment," I clarified.

"Or a divorce," Maya added.

"You're standing here telling me this wasn't planned, and you want us to believe it?" Elliott asked me at the same time Finn asked Maya, "You don't remember marrying him?"

"Bits and pieces come back to me here and there," Maya said.

I said, "Yes, you're supposed to believe it."

I looked up at the ceiling where the cherub Elvis-in-a-diaper held a violin. "For the first time in my life, I think drunk me made a decent decision."

"You just got married on accident?" Elliott asked, still disbelieving.

"Yes." I nodded. "And you can keep asking the same questions, but I've got the same answer."

"Pretty sure it was the margaritas we bought on the sidewalk," Maya added.

"They had to be spiked with something other than tequila," I agreed. "We could get some tests done."

"But I'd have to pay cash," Maya said.

"Because she's got shitty health insurance," I added. "I'll get you added to mine first thing."

Elliott wiped his thumb across his bottom lip like he did when he was about to say something that would piss me off. Then he continued to stare at me as though trying to read a playbook in French, but he didn't speak French.

"Man, what is your deal?" I asked Elliott instead of keeping my trap shut. "You wanted a distraction. I got us a distraction."

"That's not what I would've led with," Finn said, rubbing his temples. "But you do you."

"A distraction? Maya is a distraction now?" Emily asked, and the pulse in her neck was now thrumming just like her brother's.

"A questionable decision and a distraction?" Angela asked.

"That isn't what I meant. You're not only a distraction," I assured Maya with a squeeze of her hand and a sweep of my thumb along the inside of her palm.

"And you aren't only my ticket to being TikTok famous," Maya agreed, squeezing right back.

"If you hurt her." Emily pointed at me. "I'm going to ship your nuts in an unlined cardboard box to a small European country with no physicians, and I promise you, Sloan, you won't be attached to them when I do, and your health insurance will not cover the damage."

I squeezed my legs together involuntarily at this extremely specific threat.

"If you hurt her, I'll help," Angela added.

I didn't frequently encounter the consequence of castration, but I had never married Maya before either.

"We've barely walked in the door." Maya released my hand to toss her hands wide. "Can we put a pin in this and leave Sloan's testicles right where they are?"

She gestured to my aforementioned testicles, which wasn't entirely necessary. Now didn't seem like the time to bring that up, though.

"Let's listen to my wife," I said instead.

"Your wife." Elliott shook his head. "Because you married her..." Elliott confirmed this again.

"The answer is still, yes," I said.

"You married her." The guy needed to stop saying the same thing over and over.

On the outside, Elliott relatively kept his cool. He wasn't yelling, but what concerned me was how the vein in his neck pulsed. "How did I not see this coming? I should've taken you to Ohio or North Dakota or someplace you couldn't dig yourself a new hole."

"Elliott." I held up my palms in surrender. "Nobody saw this coming."

"The man's right." Finn lounged on the sofa like this wasn't a big deal at all. Everything was totally fine, and everyone needed to take a fistful of chill pills and eat a bag of Cheetos Puffs. "Mr. Denver's Most Eligible Bachelor is no longer a bachelor. The man who basically took out ads announcing the joys of single life is no longer single."

Emily glared at Finn. "What do you know about it?"

Now it was Finn's turn to throw his hands up in surrender. "Clearly, I know nothing."

"We got married! We're staying married. He didn't dump me in Lake Mead near Hoover Dam," Maya said. All the post-game marital interview questions clearly annoyed her.

"We worked it all out this morning," I added, looking directly at my new wife as I spoke.

"We communicated the hell out of the situation, and we both understand where things stand. All expectations are laid out, and this marriage will be stronger than any other because we know why we're here and exactly what the other wants out of it," Maya added, picking right up where I left off, her gaze totally locked with mine.

"Nobody's heart is involved," I said.

"It's just two people realizing that this mistake can be a mutually beneficial opportunity," she continued.

"Not only is she good for my reputation, she's not into games and bullshit," I added.

"And he's not only the reason my socials are blowing up; he also appreciates my efficiency," Maya continued.

"Elliott, you need to take a big, deep breath before you burst a blood vessel," Angela said, breaking the moment between my new wife and me.

Elliott gave her a look that had me seriously questioning if I'd missed something while I was getting drunk and getting married. Elliott, who never took direction from anyone but himself, stared right at Angela and took that deep breath she suggested.

Straight up, he was deep breathing with her, and the neck pulse thing chilled the fuck out.

New plan: I should ensure Angela was at all future negotiation meetings with Agent Elliott.

"Hey, Sloan, the guys are planning a you-got-drafted-for-marriage tailgate party for you and Maya. They're wondering if you want ribs or burgers?" Finn looked up from the screen of his cell phone.

"Are you on the team group chat?" I asked.

He nodded and asked Maya this time, "Ribs or burgers?"

"Whatever," she said. "I'm not picky. Sloan can decide."

"Uh..." I wasn't sure what I wanted. I mean, I'd made some big decisions that morning. "I think I might be out of decisions today. I don't know what to pick."

"No parties," Elliott announced. "There's a private jet meeting us on the tarmac in two hours. Finn. Sloan. You'll both pack your bags, and the plane will take you back to Denver. Sloan, you're going to huddle up in your house until I give you the all-clear to leave. You go nowhere without me. In the meantime, I'll run interference with the Stallions and social media."

Angela's phone rang. She glanced at the screen and held the phone out to Maya. "It's one of your sisters."

"Dammit." Maya pursed her lips and shook her head. "Do not answer that."

She'd turned her phone off on the way over because her sisters had a lot of thoughts about our marriage. While Maya had listened to most of them, they just kept coming.

"How about I come to Denver, too?" Maya asked, bouncing on her toes. "It's definitely time for me to get out of Vegas. Don't you think?"

I most certainly agreed. "You need extra clothes or anything?"

She shook her head. "Nope. I'm a great packer. I could live out of my suitcase for weeks."

"What about a Rookie Husband Huddle?" Finn asked, apparently still on the group chat for the team. "That seems to be in the lead for what we're gonna call this shindig."

Honestly? I liked it.

CHAPTER TWELVE

MAYA

Elliott didn't mess around—the jet arrived, and Elliott, Finn, Sloan, and I got whisked to Denver.

Angela and Emily planned to stay another day before heading back to Los Angeles. I might've felt left out, except I was on a private jet and I wasn't sure there were enough electrolytes in the world to make me feel human again.

And as soon as we landed in Denver, Elliott had a car waiting for him and Finn and another for us. Ours took us up to Sloan's house in Estes Park. We drove through town, and nothing really matched, but it all worked together with the backdrop of the mountains to create a quaint little mountain town vibe.

His house was situated off a gravel road blocked by a gate that required a code to get through. The number of swanky vehicles—Cadillacs, Porsches, Mercedes Benz—made it look like a bougie car dealership used Sloan's driveway for their overflow.

"The hell is everybody doing here?" Sloan asked as he unrolled the window of our SUV.

Our driver parked by the house—a sprawling two-story house

with a chic rustic appeal. The house had logs for siding and a stair-case that lead to the second-story front door from the driveway. The attached four-car garage with matching brown garage doors was built onto the side of the house away from view, likely so garage doors didn't mess up the front aesthetic.

There were trees everywhere—the kind with the spiky needles that made a mess all over the ground. Except, since this was the wilderness, that was probably not considered a mess, but an ambiance that helped set the tone.

Sloan unfolded himself from the SUV, his boots crunching against the gravel of the drive. I didn't do a full-body scan, though it took a full effort on my part to prevent it. What could I say? My eyes seemed to want to do it all on their lonesome.

"I'm sorry," he said, stepping toward me, palms up. "It looks like we've got a lot of company."

He should stop grinding his back teeth like that, or he was going to wish he'd married a dentist and not a backup singer.

"I like company," I assured him, hopping down from the car.

I didn't expect the cool mountain air to be soothing, but I swear it lessened the headache I'd fought all day.

"Looks like most of the team is here," he said.

I nodded. "Is now a bad time to tell you I don't really like football?"

"Maybe leave that part out when you make small talk, yeah?" he said.

Then his eyes melded with mine and lit with something... not desire. No fire. But definitely warm. Like he saw something he really liked and wanted more.

The thing was, I didn't hate that. Didn't hate how my body seemed to know his with a trust that didn't involve my head or my memory.

"What are the odds you think they've seen us? Maybe we scoot back down to Denver? Pretend we didn't come?" He glanced at his boots, then back up at me, catching my gaze from under his lashes.

"I didn't marry a man afraid to face his problems," I replied. "Remember, you're now Mr. Reliable. If Elliott says to stay put, we stay put. If there's a party? Well, yay us."

Although, if I was going to meet his entire team, I definitely would have selected alternate clothing choices. I'd also have added makeup because whatever I'd applied that morning, before we left Sin City, had probably melted off by now. Which, oh God, meant—

"I can't go in yet," I whispered.

"Okay," he said. Then he paused. "Why not?"

"I have a lip gloss situation." I'd chewed off any I'd applied on the plane. "And a shoe situation." I did. I'd worn my ratty travel sneakers and my comfiest jeans, with no less than two rips on the knees. "And a clothing situation."

There was no way a girl wore her ratties when meeting the men of the Denver Stallions football team. Honestly, I'd figured if I dressed down, then maybe it might tamp down some of the sexual energy rolling off of Sloan, colliding with mine, and creating a bomb of sexual tension.

Of note, the clothing choice hadn't achieved this. But it was worth the shot.

He looked down at my body, swallowed hard, and must've realized I was truly underdressed because he looked to the left and wouldn't meet my gaze. This would be the worst impression in the history of accidental brides.

"Your lips look great and what you're wearing is perfect," he said.

I didn't believe him one bit. Was the thin mountain air wrecking his ability to think clearly?

"Can you sneak me in the side door or something?" I didn't mean to hiss the words. "Or I can change in the car?"

That was a worst-case scenario. Ideally, I could grab my suitcase and sneak into a closet, get changed, and then I could meet everyone.

"Sloan Matthew Stevens," a gigantic mountain of a dude said from the top of the stairs. "What did you bring us home from Vegas?" He put his hand over his eyes like a visor for the sun. "Holy shit. She's real. Guys, she's real!"

"I'd like to apologize now for whatever my teammates say, do, or think in your direction." Sloan's gaze collided with mine.

That bomb I'd been hoping to diffuse with not-cute clothes threatened to detonate.

"Maya, you look great," he assured.

I made a sound like a combination of *nuh-uh* and *eep*.

He was a sweet liar.

But still a liar.

I stepped toward him and dropped my forehead to his chest. Then I lifted my head so I could repeat the motion.

Sloan didn't move out of the way or move me out of the way.

He let my head rest against his chest and wrapped his hand around the back of my neck. "One reason I love the mountains is there isn't a dress code. Wear what you like. Don't think too hard about it. Just be comfortable."

Gah, this was nice.

I leaned further into Sloan's space. Up, up, up on my toes. I didn't stop to process the way his beard scratched lightly against my cheek, only that he smelled like a wilderness retreat I'd actually enjoy.

"Did you just sniff me?" I asked against his earlobe, still close.

"Yes," he replied.

My insides got all kinds of tingly at that.

"You sniffed me first." This time, he practically nuzzled the air over my neck as he inhaled.

I was a totally melted puddle of mush.

We headed inside, and Sloan paused at the doorway to the massive living area. The walls were lighter wood than the floor, and he had a nice rug in the center of the room.

Honestly, he needed a decent amount of help with the furniture placement, but I wasn't too concerned about the furniture right then because there was a whole panel of south-facing windows that stretched from the ceiling to the floor and over-looked a totally gorgeous forest.

"Your view looks like one of the TV scenes they put on the ceiling at my dentist's office while I'm getting a cleaning," I said.

"Fuck a Ferrari. The guys worked quickly," Sloan said. "I've only been gone two days, and there's a damn balloon arch."

There was. A giant balloon arch over the door to the backyard with a sign that read: *New Husband Huddle This Way*.

"Turns out a lot can happen in twenty-four hours." I shrugged with a wry smile. "I guess we know something about that."

"We're having a party, baby," the mountain of a guy from before boomed and clapped his hands.

Things got busy then, and all the guys were smacking Sloan on the shoulder and congratulating him on the fact that I was real. I slipped off to the fringes, unsure where my place was in this whole thing.

"Married, huh?" Mountain guy strode right up to me, seeing through my attempt at disappearing into the background.

"Yup." I nodded.

"Darius." He held his hand out to me.

It engulfed mine as I shook it. "Maya."

"What'd Sloan have to pay you to agree to be his wife?" Darius asked, clearly joking. "I hope you charged extra since he grew the beard."

"Ha," I said.

While some guys were clearly fast and built for speed, Darius was built more like a tank. You might call him big boned, and you'd be right. But over those bones were a lot of freaking muscles.

"You want something to drink?" Darius asked.

"Um... do you have something with loads of electrolytes?" I asked, since I should avoid any more drinky drinks until drunk me could make better decisions.

Darius nodded and took off through the crowd, pushing through so they parted around him.

"Honest as all hell, I thought this was Finn fucking with us," he said to Sloan as he passed by. "Didn't expect her to be legitimate."

"He has a wife, and she's actually in his house." Another guy found this hysterical.

Sloan didn't seem to find it so funny, but he went along with his friends.

I took the bottle of White Raspberry ZipZing from Darius when he returned—the irony of my beverage choice not lost on me. Darius used his thumb and middle finger to whistle and get everyone's attention. Then he raised his glass. "To Maya being legit."

"To Maya being legit," everyone echoed.

"And to Denver's Most Eligible Bachelor stepping down, so I have a shot at the title!" another guy said with a huge grin. "Let's eat."

That's all it took to clear out the room, the guys all pushing and shoving on their way to the backyard.

"Hi," I said when it was only Sloan and me left alone in the gigantic space.

"Hey," he replied, glancing at my beverage with a raised eyebrow.

"It actually helps," I said. "Probably all the sugar." I dragged out the last word and winked. "How're you feeling?"

"Fine." He grinned. "Except there's too many people in my house. I think I can actively feel myself getting grouchy."

"Let's raise that blood sugar, then." I handed him the partially finished bottle.

He took the bottle, took a swig, pulled a face, then draped his arm around my shoulders.

"This place is gorgeous," I said, staring out the big wall of windows.

"My dad always talked about building a home here, a house where dreams aren't just in the imagination but possibilities waiting on the horizon," he said. "Mom and Dad never got to build here like they wanted. So, I did instead."

"Why?" I asked. "Why didn't they get to build here?" The view wasn't the reason, I already knew that.

"They died," he said, matter-of-factly. "Random accident. Nothing could've saved them. I don't like to think too much about what could've been. Not when I can't change the outcome."

"They'd be proud of you, Sloan," I said, holding his gaze as I spoke, meaning every word.

He nodded and gripped my hand as we followed the guys outside.

"Goodness," I said when we stepped out of the house and into the back.

There were more people out here—I'd guess these were the wives, girlfriends, husbands, and partners of the team.

The entire acreage was huge, but there was also a smaller patch of grass and a stone patio that wrapped around the house. On that patch of grass were tables with citronella candles and chairs covered with cream-colored cloth. Slightly darker beige bows wrapped around the backs of those chairs. A buffet table with two types of brisket, multiple types of ribs, and then skewers of roasted vegetables out the nose.

And an ice sculpture of Sloan that one guy used as a vodka luge for martinis.

With the accidental marriage, et cetera, I thought I'd had enough surprises for a lifetime. Turned out there was always room for an ice sculpture surprise.

"Darius may be a linebacker, but he also loves to throw a party," Sloan said.

Another guy—they were all blending together at that point—approached Sloan for a complicated handshake thing. "This is lit. Our little bachelor is all married, and she's not made of plastic."

"Maya, this asshole is T.J.," Sloan said. "His hobbies include fumbling the ball and making me look good just by standing there being his ugly-ass self."

83

"Guilty as charged." T.J. grinned a lopsided smile and gave me a salute instead of shaking my hand.

That was interesting. I saluted him right back.

"I take it he's one of your close friends?" I asked, given that Sloan had called him an asshole and all, but he did it with a smile.

"Damn straight," T.J. replied for Sloan.

"Ensuring I understand the dynamics." I lifted my shoulder.

"And that's what is making you an excellent wifey for Stevens." T.J. laughed like I'd told a joke.

His laugh was infectious, and I couldn't help but chuckle.

"That and the fact that now you have a shot at being Denver's most eligible bachelor," I said with a slow, sly smile.

"I like her, man. Good pick." T.J. winked at me.

"I have a question for you," Sloan said to his friend. "Did anyone even try to tell Darius this party's a bit much? Suggest something less flashy?"

"No," T.J. answered way too quickly. "Not when we all wanted to support you. See, the team is like a new jockstrap, Maya. Once we're in place, there's no stopping us from supporting what really matters."

Sloan rolled his eyes and gestured to the party. "None of you could've given me the slightest heads-up about this?"

T.J. thought for a moment. "Nope."

"You had time to get a balloon banner and an ice sculpture, but not to send a quick text? 'Hey. Sloan! Prepare for the invasion?' Nothing like that?"

"Right, right." T.J. nodded. "And you couldn't have given us the slightest heads-up you were getting married? 'Hey, guys! Prepare to meet my new wife.' Nothing like that?"

"You know what? I'm going to check out the food," I said. "Leave you two to chat this out."

I headed to the table to leave the guys to talk, loading my plate when movement at the door to the backyard caught my eye.

Finn strode through like he was ready for some serious barbecue.

Then Elliott followed, and he didn't look like he was ready to be a jockstrap kind of friend.

I didn't know who the third guy was—thin, wiry, and balding, wearing a Stallions windbreaker. But with the way everyone went quiet? He was important.

CHAPTER
THIRTEEN

SLOAN

"My job is not boring with you," Elliott said, eyes wide, taking in all that was happening in my backyard.

Football players and their plus-ones filled my normally quiet backyard. The guys all talked loudly and laughed at random shit, but their camaraderie was infectious as they playfully shoved each other around.

T.J. even attempted a backflip but didn't stick the landing. Everyone still clapped, though, because we weren't total dicks.

Elliott didn't seem impressed. "Guy is going to break his fucking wrist."

"I didn't know they were doing this," I assured.

"I knew they were doing this." Finn stood with all the self-assured-ness of a quarterback who'd just thrown for three hundred yards and three touchdowns. His grin was so wide, it could've spanned the length of the field. With hands nonchalantly tucked into pockets, he exuded an icy cool that could put a Denver snowstorm to shame.

"You were brainstorming ideas with Darius?" I asked, but also confirmed.

Finn nodded. "Hell yes. He was only going to have one kind of ribs. And who do you think suggested a damn ice sculpture?"

Well, now I knew what he'd been doing on his phone the entire way back from Vegas.

"I might've heard some rumblings," Coach McIntosh said, his gruff tone softening slightly. "Didn't think they'd execute this play so quickly. Should've known better than to underestimate these boys when there's chow involved."

"You've got to have more faith in us, Coach," Finn said. Then he jerked his thumb toward the buffet. "But since there's barbecue, I'm gonna..." He trailed off, already making his way toward the spread.

I closed my eyes, preparing to get reamed for the party. "I didn't know this party was happening; I would've told them to stop—"

"Look, kid, if poor decisions won games, then you'd be in the Hall of Fame with the way you single-handedly got ZipZing to pull all their cash." Coach had no problem interrupting me.

With a deep breath, I straightened my posture and put on a confident smile. "Fucked up on that one, I admit."

There was an unmistakable twinkle hidden beneath Coach's gruff exterior. "Management loves that you latched on a ball and chain, so people are talking about *that* instead of the mother-fucking sugar content. You might be some sort of gridiron genius if you can actually execute this publicity play and secure that contract extension." He paused dramatically before adding with a dry chuckle, "Now, my job is to ensure your head stays on the field, and you didn't leave it in some Vegas wedding chapel."

"Marriage won't affect my game," I assured. *What the hell am I gonna do if I can't play the game?*

"This is your Hail Mary pass in the last quarter," Elliott said.

"I've got this," I said with more confidence than I felt.

"Have you seen what they're calling the two of you?" Elliott asked. "Your official 'super couple' name?"

"Sloan and Maya?" I countered because that's what I'd expected they'd call us.

"Slaya." Elliott let that set in.

Honestly, I liked it. "I can live with that."

"You know, I thought this was stupid. But this marriage charade might be the breakthrough you need to get some good press for a change," Elliott continued, his voice low, as if sharing a secret. "But it could also be your downfall if you fuck it up."

"It's not a charade," I declared firmly, meeting his gaze head on.

He raised an eyebrow in warning, a silent reminder of the delicate balance I treaded.

As I made my way over to the buffet table, Finn greeted me with a plate piled high with ribs and brisket.

"Come on, dig in," he urged, his eyes glinting mischievously.

I took my plate and glanced around to find Maya. Where was Maya?

"Did anyone see where my wife went?" I asked the question that a day ago, I never thought I'd be asking. Honestly, it tasted odd, but in a good way.

I found her sitting with Darius and his long-term girlfriend Nisha. T.J. had parked his ass with them, too.

Maya caught my eye and flashed a radiant smile that made me want to slide my hand in hers. Steal her away to some place where it'd be just the two of us.

But I didn't.

Instead, I took a seat beside her, and my hand found hers all on its own. Chemistry was doing its natural thing, lighting a fire on muscle memory.

"You gonna move down to the city or keep Maya here all to yourself?" Darius asked, shoveling in the barbecue.

Well, this was my spot. My backyard was the place I came with a beer or a cup of coffee while I waited for the deer to come through.

Still, I took a moment to consider Darius' question before replying, my eyes wandering over the landscape beyond the backyard.

The flow of the water and the occasional rustle of leaves gave me a peace I didn't find anywhere else.

"Not leaving this place," I admitted, letting go of Maya's hand so I could eat. "But Maya and I will figure things out together. We're still new, you know?"

I loved this property. It wasn't the smaller house I grew up in down the way. This was the house Dad always meant to build but never got to.

Pictures of my parents flickered through my mind like they always did if I let them. They had always been my biggest support from the sidelines since the first time I ever stepped on the field. But their voices went silent right before I got drafted into the national league. The single-most stable thing in my life was gone in an instant. One second, they were planning their dream home; the next, a totally avoidable car accident robbed them of seeing their only kid's dream of playing pro happen.

Eventually, the Stallions became my surrogate family.

"I don't really do outside," Maya said, wrinkling her nose. "I mean, it's stunning here, but I'm a city girl."

"What do you mean, you don't do outside?" I asked.

"I prefer air conditioning and heat and filtered water."

"You never camp?" I asked. "Hike?"

"God, no. Why would I sleep outside when there's so many more comfortable places inside?" she asked, grimacing. "Or walk where there're no bathrooms?"

"I know I couldn't do the mountains," Nisha agreed. "Not with all the bugs and stuff." She shivered.

"There are rabbits and birds and squirrels," T.J. said, glancing around. "They're cute."

"Ladies love shit like that," Darius added.

"What do you know about what ladies love?" Nisha asked, poking Darius in the ribs.

"Oh, I think I've got a good idea," he said, lifting his eyebrows.

"Nope. Those cute little things get eaten by *bigger* things," Nisha said, pointing her fork in T.J.'s direction.

Maya's smile faltered slightly, her gaze flicking toward the dense tree line. "I mean... Denver's not that far if we found a place there. It's closer to the team."

T.J. opened his mouth and started to say, "Oh, he's got—"

"It's safe up here. We've got bug spray for the tiny stuff and nothing big comes near the house." I reached for her hand, giving it a reassuring squeeze.

"Usually," Darius so unhelpfully added. "It's safe, usually."

"Stay inside to be sure," Nisha advised.

I wanted to keep the mood light, to ease the tension obviously building in Maya.

"We have deer over at the creek." I pointed to the direction where the deer came through. "It's peaceful to watch them in the early morning when the sun's rising over that ridge right there."

"I don't really do early," Maya said. "I'm more of a late-at-night kind of person."

"Do not go outside at night," Nisha said, shaking her head.

"You don't do early?" I asked. "Some of the best things happen when everything's fresh."

"Uh... no." Maya shook her head. "Those things can happen while I sleep."

"Do you two even know each other?" Darius asked because he wanted to piss me off.

"I'll introduce you to the deer. You'll love them," I assured Maya while side-eyeing Darius.

"Okay, Cinderella," Darius said with a laugh.

I willed Darius to close his mouth. Dude gave a great party, but he didn't know when to stop talking. "I am not fucking Cinderella. I ended up with property that runs along a deer trail. I like it, and the deer don't seem to mind, either." I turned to Maya. "It'll grow on you. Promise."

"Girl, don't let him fool you. Where there is prey, there are predators." Nisha pointed two fingers at her eyes, then at Maya. "You get me?"

As if on cue, a rustling in the bushes nearby caught our attention. Maya seemed to naturally move in as she clutched my arm.

Finn emerged from the other side of the bushes, and Maya made a small *meep* noise.

"That is just your friendly neighborhood player," I said, pointing toward him. "That's the only thing you have to worry about around here."

"Trust me," Darius added, laughing. "He's not wrong."

CHAPTER
FOURTEEN

SLOAN

Once we got the topic off of mountain shit, Maya fit right in with the team. It wasn't unexpected, but I dug it all the same.

After the guys cleaned up, and we saw them off, Maya started pushing furniture around the living room, staring at it, then pushing it someplace else. I didn't know what she was doing, but I wouldn't let my wife do the heavy lifting, so I helped.

We were on the fourth placement of the sofa.

"Now, when you sit there, you can see the big windows, and when you sit there, you can watch television, and if you sit all the way over here, you have a perfect view of the kitchen." She finally —thank fuck—nodded at the placement.

"Is it always like this for you with the team?" she asked.

"Sorry?" I asked.

"This… busy?" Maya asked, studying the sofa from another angle.

"It's a different busy during the season. I do have an apartment in the city if I need it. Or if you need it." I hoped she wouldn't need it. "During the off-season, I like it better up here in the mountains.

Despite all their talk, the guys come up a lot since it's so quiet here." I paused. "Quiet until they show up, anyway."

"I get it." She nodded, and her eyes softened, as though she really got it. "Needing some space. And this place up here... even just the inside? It's worth the drive."

"Are we done moving the furniture?" I asked. "Or are you thinking we might try the sofa in the kitchen?"

I'd hired a decorator to come in and arrange all this for me when we closed escrow. I hadn't thought twice about how she'd laid it out—figured that was her job, not mine.

Maya laughed and squeezed my arm. "The sofa placement is finally perfection."

I mean, I could move furniture all night if we had to, but there were lots of other things I'd rather be doing. She'd mentioned her love of sex. And I'd agreed that I also enjoyed sex.

And now, we were here alone, and there were all kinds of surfaces to use. Like that sofa—that could be fun. We could pile the pillows and—

"The couch is okay, but the rug isn't centered," she said, hustling to yank one of the rugs into a new placement below the windows.

God, she was pretty.

Blood flow had gone south when she'd bent over to move the rug, so I needed a minute to scoop all the bits back together in my brain. Then I'd be good for conversation again.

We were rearranging furniture, but my body didn't care. The pull to move to her and touch her was magnetic.

"I didn't say it, but you know that if you need anything here, you can help yourself." Not that I needed to vocalize this. She'd already been moving the furniture around, and had re-organized the closet, so there was all kinds of space for her stuff.

"I know, I've had like four ZipZings," she said. "For a guy who ticked them off, you sure have a lot."

Yeah, cases of the stuff came with the initial endorsement deal.

"You had four?" Along with all the sugar, those things had loads of caffeine.

"Good news. I have zero hangover left. I think they cured it," she said.

I bet they did.

"Well, anything else you need? You go ahead and take it," I said.

"Anything?" she asked, absolutely checking me out with a full body scan.

The little twitch at the edges of her lips? Oh yes, she liked what she saw. And so did I.

"Anything," I agreed, giving her the same look right back.

Look at me, flirting with my new wife.

Maya offered a genuine grin. Not the fake one I'd noted she sometimes pinned to her lips. This one was the real deal.

"I was thinking—" I said.

"You know what would be fun—"

That magnetic pull took over, and she took a step toward me, her eyes locked with mine. I took a step toward her, still holding her gaze.

Another step from her, and the play was in motion on the field, and nobody cared where the rugs were.

I moved forward toward her with no direction from my brain. My body was doing it all by itself. Like a magnet, she met me halfway.

The air between us shifted.

"We're alone," I said, lifting my hand to her cheek.

"And the flow of traffic for your living room is going to work so much better." She nodded and with the motion, she doubled down on the hand-to-cheek scenario.

"Moving furniture turns you on?" I asked, mostly joking.

"An organized room is always a turn on," she agreed. "Have you ever had a blow job in front of that window?"

Um… "That one specifically?"

She waited for my answer.

"No," I said with a sly smile.

Maya gripped at my shirt and held on. Was she holding on to keep her balance or so I wouldn't slip away?

"You know, legally, we can do what we want." Was she flirting with me, too? She totally was.

"No one could stop us." I lifted my index finger and traced the apple of her cheek, trailing it around to tuck a piece of her hair behind her ear.

Her pupils dilated, and her lips parted.

"Sloan," she said my name and nothing else.

Sometimes in a guy's life, things didn't seem natural. When I had to give direction to my body to move here or go there or pay attention to this or that thing. But in that moment, my body moved of its own accord. Understood precisely what to do with no direction.

"I'm going to kiss you," I said.

"Where?" she asked, quirking a brow.

"Everywhere." I leaned in and brushed my lips against hers. Light. Nothing serious, only enough to test the waters.

She pulled me closer, repeating the gesture on my lips.

"Have you ever had a guy go down on you in front of that window?" I asked, mirroring her question.

"That window, specifically?" she asked, tilting her head to the side.

My brain didn't compute the joke at first. I was already hard, and my blood wasn't flowing like usual.

"I'm going to listen to you come and know that I'm the one bringing you there," I said.

"You should do that," Maya said. "It'd be my first time."

"In front of that window?" I asked.

"Uh-huh." Her mouth was on mine, her hands in my hair.

God, but I wanted to lay her on that couch we'd moved, touch her everywhere. Use my tongue and taste her. Feel her body against mine and remember every fucking second.

"I want you so bad it hurts." It physically fucking hurt.

"Then you should do something about it." Her hand was already undoing the fly on my jeans.

I kissed her—pressed my mouth to hers and rolled her onto her back along the cushions of the sofa facing the window.

Her mouth moved against mine, and her hands roamed along the ridges of my back. I moved back only long enough to pull my shirt over my head. Then my mouth was back on hers, hands roaming everywhere.

My fingers trailed up her abdomen, along the side of her belly, to her breasts. The tight buds of her nipples stood pert and hard. I traced the pad of my thumb over one, then the other.

She moaned and arched up into my hand. Her hands gripped my shoulders like she was afraid I would disappear.

But that wouldn't happen.

"Shirt off," I said.

She groaned and pulled away from me but clearly enjoyed the direction. I allowed her to move away to remove her shirt, tracing her other nipple as she moved away.

With a quick motion, she removed her shirt, and without being asked, she shimmied her pants and underwear down to her ankles and kicked them off.

"Pants off." She countered my demand with one of her own, and, hell yes, I got off on that.

I pulled off my underwear and shorts, my hard dick practically rejoicing in being removed from the cotton restraints.

Her hand moved to me, and she stroked once, twice, then used her thumb between the crevice at the tip.

My dick jumped in her hand, ready to do whatever she asked of me.

But I got to play, too, and if she kept that grip with the up and down motion, the swirl and press of her thumb over the top of my shaft, then things would end entirely too soon. I'd be embarrassed.

But then I'd get to go down on her to finish things off.

Not that the latter would be a hardship. Not at all. "When you come, I'm going to be inside you."

She made a strangled sound in the back of her throat and pulled my mouth harder against hers.

I pressed up over the top of her and savored the feel of my bare chest against hers. Her bare breasts, full and heavy, pressed up against my pecs.

She groaned and pressed her wet center against my thigh.

"You don't know what you do to me," I murmured against her temple.

Neither of us could say anything after that because our lips and mouths moved against each other. Tongues darting and tasting, lips pressing, brushing… savoring.

She parted her legs, making room for me there. The tip of me nudged the damp warmth of her, bringing me back to the present.

"Condom, baby," I said against her mouth. "Gotta get a condom."

I wanted to push inside her body and have it all, but after the chaos of the morning, the last thing I wanted was for either of us to have regrets. Any regrets.

The quickest way to regret was to do something regrettable.

Fuck it, I'd never been a poet.

She moaned a low groan but released her tight grip on me. "On the pill. I'm on the pill."

"I'm clean," I assured.

"Me, too," she said.

Careful not to give her too much of my weight, I moved down her body—licking and tasting all along the way. Brushing butterfly kisses to the side of her breasts, down her abdomen, along her hip, to the apex of her thighs, and farther down to her knees, ankles, even toes. Then I worked my way back up.

"This okay?" I asked, checking in because my body might know hers, but the rest of me was still learning.

She answered without speaking, pulling me to her in answer while groaning something that sounded like a yes.

Both of us naked, we made out like this was all we'd ever have.

And if it was all we had, then by hell we would milk it for all it was worth.

My erection ached, blood thrummed, and my body demanded more. But I wasn't in a rush anymore because this position allowed my fingers to trail between her legs and explore the warmth there. Gently, I slipped one finger inside.

"Sloan," she said my name like it meant everything to her. Like I was all that mattered.

A guy could get off on that.

She tried to grind against my hand, but there was no way for her to gain traction in this position. Given that I was a nice guy, I handled that for her—pressing my finger against the rough bundle of nerves near the front of her opening.

"Yes." She moved against my hand, clenching her internal muscles around my finger in a way that made my dick seriously jealous.

I pressed my finger in and out, trailing over the spot I knew would make her wild, until the primed muscles inside nearly came on my hand.

That's when I stopped.

Because I had a plan.

Eyes glassy, she reached for my hand. "Don't stop."

"Trust me," I said, kissing each of her fingers before moving along to her wrist, then her elbow, then down her belly.

Using my tongue until she arched off the cushions.

Her breaths came quicker, and I had to press my hips into the couch to relieve some of the pressure in my groin.

And then I ate. She clearly dug it. This was obvious both from the sounds she made and from the way her fingers threaded in my hair to push my tongue deeper.

I got her right to the edge again, her internal muscles tight and ready.

Then I stopped.

She let out a garbled cry as I sat—ass to ankles—and stroked myself, enjoying the view. Then I was over the top of her, aligned with her body, my erection pressing into the space between her thighs.

I threaded my gaze with hers, letting them mingle with anticipation, waiting for her to give me the green light that she was still good with this.

She reached with her thumb to trace the bottom of my lip. "Yes, Sloan."

That's all the permission I needed. Gently seating myself inside her, I reveled in the feeling of her tight warmth wrapped around the hard length of me.

I never broke the thread of our gazes, keeping track of her, ensuring things were still working for her.

Her eyes went wide when I buried myself to the hilt, so I stilled, letting her adjust to me, until she nudged me on with her hips.

Wet and ready and mine, I thrust inside and pulled nearly out. Then on repeat. All while murmuring how gorgeous she was, how perfect she felt, how amazing I thought she was, until her breathing shifted and she made a little mewl right before she climaxed.

I kept the tempo steady, but when her muscles clenched around me, I let myself fall along with her. Letting out a growl or a roar, or maybe both? It was hard to tell who made which noises.

Even as the aftershocks subsided, she didn't release her grip on me. Holding me against her. Her face buried in my neck.

"I think I'm still coming," she said, against my skin. "How did you...?"

I would've moved so we could see each other, but she still had that killer grip on me and after coming like that, I couldn't find the strength to move.

"Delayed gratification," I said into the couch cushion.

She loosened her grip on me so I could roll over—my side to her front.

"Next time, let me come the first time, so you don't have to wait," she whispered with a sly smile.

"Baby, you're mine, and that means you'll come when I'm ready for you to come," I said.

"You're good at this," she announced.

That was a compliment, so I'd take it. "Thanks."

"I don't just mean the sex part—although you are exceptional at that. I mean, total gold-star worthy."

She seemed so serious with this declaration that I couldn't help it. I grinned.

"I mean the rest of it, too. The whole gig here. You're good at the whole attentive thing."

"Okay," I said, because I wasn't sure what a guy was supposed to say to that. She made it easy. It's not like I had to try.

We lay there together, tangling and untangling our hands while staring outside. I lost myself in the landscape stretching beyond the window.

Maya's voice was soft and inviting as she said, "This place means a lot to you, doesn't it?"

I nodded. "It's more than just land and a house," I began, my voice barely above a whisper.

"This place is your Las Vegas at night, isn't it?" she asked, facing me, brushing the hair away from my forehead. "It's your field during a game."

"It's my stage once the concert starts," I added, nodding.

Maya's presence was a comforting warmth against the cold I'd felt only seconds earlier. I hadn't realized the warmth was missing in this place until that moment.

"Thank you for sharing it with me," she said.

We lay there together, letting that be enough.

"You think you can sleep?" I asked.

She nodded. "You?"

This time, I nodded.

"Let's get some sleep?" she asked, like there was a shot in hell I didn't plan on tasting her again before morning.

But then she yawned, so I knew I should let her rest first.

"Yeah," I said.

Swear to fuck, she purred.

Then I carried her to bed, pulled my wife into my arms, and let myself savor my new reality.

CHAPTER
FIFTEEN

MAYA

Of course, Sloan's comfortable bed wasn't a surprise. The guy definitely embodied a comfortable life, what with all the flannel.

His desire for comfort wasn't ever in question. No, his investment in high thread count sheets was the surprise. Honestly, I expected comfy flannel sheets. That seemed more on brand for him.

But nope. He had one-thousand-plus thread counts of the good stuff. I could respect a man who invested in good bedding.

I pressed my face into the pillow and inhaled the scent of Sloan.

Things were quiet up here in the mountains. Too quiet, given the number of bugs and deer hanging around outside.

Still, Sloan's even breaths and my tossing and turning were the only sounds. Sometimes I'd hear the low buzzing of an insect, but it didn't get close, so I didn't worry too much. Only a little.

No street lights. Not even a porch light to break through the inky darkness—Sloan had flicked that off earlier.

My hangover was long gone, but those ZipZings were no joke. There was no way I would sleep after four.

He slept soundly beside me with a look of innocence that was totally unfair, because dear Lord in heaven, the man knew how to use his body to please mine.

Flipping on my back, I stared at the shiplap ceiling.

I should get up.

It might be the middle of the night, but I wouldn't be getting any sleep. So, yes, I should get up. Of everything I knew, this was the most certain step. Cautiously, not to make the floorboards creek, I rolled out of bed and tiptoed to the shower.

His bathroom was small but functional. A guy clearly lived there, because while tidy, it wasn't spotless. The little hairs on the edge of the sink would drive a person nuts after a while. And though the room was utilitarian—lacking the little touches of someone who would appreciate it for more than simple everyday use—I wouldn't change anything about it.

Blowing out a breath, I showered, then I headed downstairs to the kitchen to see if Sloan had some ice cream, or chocolate, or even cookies. I hit pay dirt behind the expired bag of Doritos in the cupboard in an unopened box of Oreos.

The expired Doritos gave me pause—who didn't finish them before they expired? And the unopened Oreos? Sacrilege.

I peeled the blue cellophane Oreo bag open and grabbed a cookie. I bit. Then I spat.

Stale.

I tossed the mess into the trash, including the cookies and the expired chips. Then I fished everything out of the cupboard—all the canned goods and pantry staples, organizing them by category and then expiration.

The layout Sloan used for the pantry and kitchen didn't make a bit of sense.

His glasses weren't anywhere near the sink, so I remedied that. The pots and pans were all the way on the other side of the kitchen from the stove, so I fixed that, too.

I didn't mean to sing as I worked, it just happened. There in the kitchen, with the massive vaulted ceilings, the acoustics were spot on. My voice bounced off the walls and filled the kitchen. The high ceilings were incredible, turning my simple song into a sound that wrapped around me like an embrace.

As I sang one of the cover songs for the artist headlining my last tour, I got lost in the music. I swayed to the rhythm, letting it carry me away. The music lifted something inside me, untangling knots that even an organized pantry couldn't fix.

On the lingering echoes of my song, I checked to see if the table might fit against the wall with the window so we could look outside while we ate breakfast instead of into the living room— that would save us from having to stand and drink coffee to look outside.

It took a bit of maneuvering. But, good news, the table fit.

I lifted the binoculars he'd left there by the window. Oh, these had a night vision setting. How bananas was that? Pressing them against my eyelids, it took a moment to adjust to the greenish-black haze of figures.

But then something moved, and my heart rate ticked up as the bushes rustled. I squinted. Whatever creature this was, it wasn't a bug.

I seriously hoped they didn't have bugs that big here, anyway.

I scanned the yard, stopping at trash cans near where the rustling had happened, and there was movement. Holy crap, too big to be a deer. Here's the thing: Even though I was a city girl, I was pretty sure that was a bear.

I screeched a sound that wasn't quite a scream, but also not nothing either.

And the bear was outside.

I was inside.

But with the binoculars, it felt like we were both inside. This was the only reason I backed up and hit my hip on the edge of the table. This wouldn't have happened if I'd left it where it'd been.

When I took out my hip on the edge of the table, I swear the bear looked up. If it weren't so dark, we would've made eye contact.

This time, I did scream. I wasn't proud of it, but it happened.

The bear seemed to freeze in place. I dropped the binoculars to the table—thank goodness it was right there—

"Sloan!" I yelled. "Sloan!"

He didn't come immediately, so I started up the stairs to find him, still calling for him the entire way. He met me at the top of the stairs in nothing but a pair of boxers and socks.

The guy either wore socks after sex, or he put them on to come save me—either way, I wasn't so sure about that.

"There is a bear. There is a bear." I pointed in the general direction of the backyard. "There i-i-i-s a bear. I think it was a black bear, but it's night, so maybe it's brown. I'm pretty sure it wasn't a polar bear since we're not in the Arctic."

The blinking thing he did was kinda cute if there hadn't been a bear ready to come at us through the kitchen window.

"Is it in the house?" He looked behind me, apparently not too concerned about Mr. Bear.

"No." I shook my head. "Why would it be in the house?"

"Then he's where he's supposed to be," he said, still groggy. "The guys probably didn't tie down the trash can lids. It happens."

"Are you kidding me right now?" I asked. "There's a bear, Sloan. It's a bear."

"Let me look." He scratched at his jaw as he moved past me to the kitchen.

I should've explained what had happened in there, since I was still mid-rearranging and at the part where everything looked worse than it was, with the contents of the cabinets spread over the counters and such.

He made it to the kitchen and stared at the mess for a long pause. He glanced at me and lifted an eyebrow. "Was the bear in the kitchen?"

"This is all me. I just wanted a cookie. And then I found the Oreos. Then this happened." I gritted my teeth, hoping like hell he wouldn't be angry. "This is what tests an accidental marriage, you know? But don't think too much about it. It'll be perfect when I'm done." I pushed my knuckles against my mouth.

Now was a good time to stop talking.

"I have Oreos?" he asked, frowning. "Where?"

"I tossed 'em." I pointed to a bag of expired food. There were two big garbage bags full of expired pantry items. "They'd gone stale."

He blinked hard at the trash sacks.

"But the, uh, bear. He's right out there by the... you know." I handed him his binoculars, nudging him toward the window.

He took a peek. Looked around thoroughly.

"Nothin' is out there," he said, finally.

"No, he's there." I crossed my heart. "Promise."

"Okay." He set down his binoculars and promptly walked into the edge of the table. "Ow."

"I know. I did the same thing," I said. "You'll get used to the new placement."

He paused, rubbing his thigh. I should motor on back to bed and pretend none of this had happened. I didn't. Instead, I simply watched my husband.

"Whatever it was, it's gone," he assured, handing me the binoculars to see for myself.

I took the binoculars and peeked.

He was right, though the trash can with the bushes right behind it and that branch right there looked a whole lot like a... bear.

"I think I saw the trash cans," I said, deflated, setting the binoculars down and glancing sheepishly at him.

"I don't know what I'm supposed to do right now to protect you from the trash cans." He fixed his eyes only on me, not the wreck of a mess I'd left behind.

"Well, don't leave me here alone. There could be all sorts of animals that show up." I didn't have a lot of requests, just that one.

He stepped forward, tracing his fingertip along my arm. "Nothing's getting in the house."

I actually believed him. I was safe here. I pressed my palms to his chest and stepped into his embrace.

"I'm going to kiss you. You good with that?" he asked.

"Uh, yes?" I sort of said, sort of asked. Then leaned back and gestured to my mouth.

He did as he promised, kissing me until I wasn't thinking at all about the wildlife. Somehow, he had backed me up the stairs, and oh, yes, yes, yes, Maybe I didn't need midnight organization when I could have... this.

But then he lifted me up. I was in his arms, his mouth was against mine, and finally, I was in the bed, and he was... tucking me in?

What the hell just happened?

I peeled open my eyes as he tucked the bedding around me.

"You need sleep, baby," he said against my mouth before he climbed into bed next to me. "It's been a long day."

That's how I found myself once again in his bed, thinking about his sheets. I had to stop thinking about Sloan's bedding.

Unfortunately, my brain would shut none of that off.

I tossed. I turned.

"You're not sleeping," Sloan said from the darkness.

I swallowed against my dry throat. "No." I nearly asked, 'Are you?' But that would've been silly given that he was obviously awake.

"I can't sleep either," he said.

I turned toward the direction of his voice, pulling the sheet and comforter with me. "Too much in your head?"

He chuckled, a low, deep rumble down in his throat, and he reached for me, pulling me to him.

"There's a lot to think about." His words came gravelly and raspy and oddly delicious. Like I could taste them—which was silly because they were words. Even so, my taste buds flooded with caramel, vanilla, and warm spice. Nutmeg or cinnamon or something like that.

I wondered if my words had a flavor for him.

"I promise I'll get your kitchen fixed tomorrow." I would've crossed my heart, but I couldn't while pressed against him and all.

"Go to sleep, Maya," he said, with a low, caramel-laced chuckle.

I liked that—the way I could practically see his lips twitching even with my face buried in his chest.

"G'night, Sloan," I said.

And even with all the danger outside, I knew I was safe here with him.

That's when I finally fell asleep.

The sun was just beginning to filter through the curtains when I woke up, disoriented by the warmth in Sloan's embrace.

I started to shift away, but he pulled me closer, murmuring something in his sleep that sounded like "stay."

How could I say no to that? I turned back to face him, pressing a soft kiss to his cheek before settling back into his arms.

CHAPTER
SIXTEEN

MAYA

Time was an odd thing when I was with Sloan—it went fast and slow all at once. Like a river that was calm and steady on the surface, but underneath the currents raged with an unseen force. I mean, it'd only been a few weeks, but it felt like we'd been together for ages. We just... fit. And when we didn't fit, we discussed it and released old expectations by setting new ones. This whole thing made no sense to me because the rhythm we found with each other seemed too perfect to be real.

Yes, I had doubts about this situation-ship we'd agreed on. I had a hard time calling it a relationship when every relationship I'd ever been in came to an abrupt stop before now. The rain always brought the mud... but not with Sloan.

I swallowed hard, because the last time I felt this content, I promptly got served with divorce papers. That was two weeks after Dan and I had said, 'I do.'

But there had been signs with that marriage. We didn't talk, hardly at all. Actually, we communicated more after he handed me the divorce papers than we'd ever done during the 'marriage.'

But that wasn't this, and Dan wasn't Sloan. Sloan wasn't my

first husband, either, or any of the other number of boyfriends I'd had through the years.

I shoved all of those thoughts deep, deep down and forced myself to remember that I had to live for today and the present.

Was this real? Did communicating the hell out of this marriage and laying out all expectations actually mean it would work?

Or was it only buying us slightly more time in the raft on the river of time? Were we only fooling ourselves, or was this real? And how did a person figure it out before anyone got hurt?

Those were the questions, weren't they? Questions that didn't have answers.

I took extra time with my makeup that morning since I planned to film a few more reels for social media. There was one hickey at the base of my neck that needed extra coverage, so I selected a green mock-turtleneck shirt to go with my black high-waisted pants. The ones with the pleated front and a little split at the ankles. The whole vibe was chic-mountain with cutesy flip-flops. Perfect for a musician on the rise.

My social media accounts continued to grow, and 'Slaya' became a trending hashtag.

I finished up and trotted down the stairs, pausing at the hall closet, which was mid-organization. Meaning it was currently a disaster but on the way to completion. This was my favorite part. Cleaning up the mess I'd made and proving to myself it wasn't for nothing.

No Sloan around, but dang, I had a system for these things—and I knew the system—but with no idea of what the system entailed, Sloan must've thought I was bonkers.

In our last Salt and Pepper Negotiations, I assured him I would finish all organizational projects within twenty-four hours—barring any illness, natural disasters, or wildlife.

A Salt and Pepper Negotiation was what we called it when one of us needed to cover something important. That way, we both knew what was up and there was no guessing involved for either of us.

"Sloan?" I called his name, ready to apologize for the gigantic mess of the hall closet.

No reply, but a note taped to the coffee maker caught my eye:

Out of coffee.
Walked to town to grab a cup.
Will bring yours back.
- S

I laughed lightly. At nothing. I laughed at nothing and everything that had happened since we got margaritas in Vegas.

Colorado was absolutely not Vegas, though. This wasn't the desert, and there were no flashing lights or pretend lakes.

Everything here was the real deal. I'd found that refreshing.

Mountain air was interesting, because with the fog that settled, it was wet and faded the edges of the landscape, but somehow, things still felt crisp. Awake and alive and happy.

I texted a jaunty good morning to my friends, asking for a check in. I got one thumbs up and one goose gif in reply.

Grabbing the guitar I'd had shipped in from Los Angeles, I pulled the strap over my shoulder and checked to ensure it was tuned. I hadn't turned on my camera to record.

I always posted covers of already popular songs. But since I was alone, and the acoustics in this room were so damn good, I decided on the fly to try out one of my originals. Letting my hair spill over my shoulder, I worked on the melody that had been in my head since I came up with the lyrics.

Once I could nail the bridge, the rest of the song fell into place.

I don't love you, but I'm yours.
You don't need me, but you're mine.
When I feel you, I know the truth.
In life, it's those things that aren't real

Those things that become how I feel.

I wanted the song to be raw and honest, but somehow, whenever I put pen to paper, it always felt like the chords weren't quite right.

That's why I stuck with the tried-and-true songs others wrote —those always worked.

But by myself in the big room, the usual worry about what others would think of my words fell away like a heavy coat sliding from my shoulders. I closed my eyes, lost in my music, and let the emotion pour.

I closed my eyes, the music flowed, and it was only me and the song. When I strummed the last chord, and soft applause broke the silence, I opened my eyes to find Sloan there, his expression one of pride.

"You wrote that?" Sloan's voice was barely above a whisper, as if speaking too loudly would shatter the fragile moment we found ourselves in.

"Uh-huh. I've been…uh…working on trying something new," I said, hastily putting my guitar to the side. "Yay, coffee!"

He handed it over, letting his fingertips brush mine. We'd both discovered we enjoyed little touches, so we wove that into the fabric of our agreement.

Then he leaned in and pressed a gentle kiss against my temple. I liked when he did that, so I should add that to our agreement, too. The next time we opened up for negotiations, anyway.

"I meant to apologize about the hall closet. I got tired and—"

"You are well within the agreed-upon timeframe," he said. "And even if you weren't, I won't complain about being able to find towels." He glanced at the guitar, then back at me. "Your song was—"

"Just a song." I lifted the cup to my lips.

He sat next to me on the sofa. Not too close, but close enough that I could catch his scent and appreciate the way his lips moved under the beard.

I...uh...had many reasons for preferring the beard at this point. Most of them were inappropriate to bring up, but I'd also added keeping the facial hair to our agreement.

"You realize that, more than everyone I've ever met, you're always moving?" he asked.

When we sat together like this, he lounged back and crossed an ankle over his knee. But today, he didn't do that. No, he was all focused on me.

"Always moving?" I asked with a self-deprecating chuckle. "Walking in circles, sure."

"Don't do that." He shook his head, one of his fingers toying with the edge of my hair where it rested along my shoulder. "Don't put my wife down like that."

"Oh, come on, you've known me for less than a minute." I meant the words as a joke, but they didn't work. Actually, they seemed to touch a nerve because he pursed his lips and glanced away.

"The only person to determine if you're going forward or backward is you," Sloan said in all seriousness. "All movement is technically the same. Whether you run up the field or down, it's all part of the journey. That journey is taking you forward, either way."

"That all sounds very sage, but until you came into my life, I only found myself in the same spot over and over." It was the truth. Always a new tour, always in the background. Taking a paycheck and then onto the next.

"And now, you're moving forward."

"I'm living in Vegas at night," I said with a smile. I was, and it was amazing.

"Can I post this?" he asked, holding his phone for me to see. "On my socials this time?" He handed over his phone, open to the video recording app.

"You recorded me?" I asked, taking the phone, my hands a

touch shaky because I wasn't certain I wanted to see what he'd filmed.

I was there, so I knew what had happened and how it went. I set the cup of coffee on the ottoman and stared at the still image of me on the screen with my guitar.

I didn't love the idea of telling him no. But I disliked the idea of him posting my flop of a song more.

"Just look," he suggested, nodding to the screen.

I pushed play.

The sun was shining behind me through the big windows, casting a golden glow over everything it touched as I sang the lyrics.

Funny that from this point of view—the view outside my head —they sounded amazing. The emotion came through so strongly, and the lyrics reverberated off the walls in a way that melded with the acoustic guitar, adding poignancy I hadn't realized was there.

"They don't sound like that in my head," I said, peering closer at the screen.

The fits and starts and pauses as I sorted the bridge actually made the song more intimate. I glanced at Sloan, and his eyes filled with pride and admiration.

"Okay," I decided on the spot. "You can post, but...gah... maybe not?" I ran my hand over my hair. "I mean, I could do it again, and it could be better. Not so many stops and starts, you know?"

"Then it wouldn't be Vegas at night," he said.

Funny enough, I understood exactly what he meant. If I made it perfect, it would lose the perfection.

So, I nodded, bit my lip, and made myself say, "Post it."

CHAPTER
SEVENTEEN

SLOAN

Relationships sucked. But it turned out that the problem with every relationship I'd ever been in was that I wasn't married.

Or maybe it was because those partners weren't Maya.

The video I posted of her got reposted by most of the guys on the team, and then it blew the fuck up. Her song was everywhere. She went from TikTok famous to straight-up a big fucking deal.

Maya's online success only continued to grow after that reel of her own music went mega-viral. Her original songs all bypassed the covers she'd done before. And she continued to post them. Each one gained more attention than the last. I couldn't keep up with the number of likes, views, and shares she had. There were entirely too many to count.

"What do I even do with all of this attention?" Maya said, pacing in the bedroom with a purple bottle of ZipZing in her hand.

I tried to focus on packing for training camp, but the weight of her uncertainty was palpable. As she continued to pace, her footsteps echoed in the room, in contrast to the silence that followed her question. Maya only paused her pacing to watch me toss in a pair of shorts and a tube of toothpaste.

I turned to look at her, her expression a mix of concern and apprehension.

"You keep being you," I said, ensuring my words were heavy with reassurance. "You've got something special. You've got a gift."

Maya's eyes met mine, a whole heap of emotions swirling within them. And then, without warning, she strode straight to me, set the bottle on the dresser, and threw her arms around me in a fierce hug. I pulled her into a tight embrace, her heartbeat thudding against mine.

She pulled back slightly. Our gazes locked.

"I'm just scared," she confessed softly, her vulnerability shining through the facade of confidence. Her fingertips grazed my jawline, her touch gentle.

I cupped her face in my hands, my thumbs tracing small circles on her cheeks.

"If you're scared, then I'm here to be scared with you," I whispered. "But, Maya, I have to be honest. If you keep pressing against me like this, I'll never make it to training camp, and then Coach is gonna be furious. I won't get a contract extension, and that won't turn out well for anyone."

She laughed, pulling away to survey my bag.

"Is that how you're doing it?" she asked, frowning. "You know you can fit so much more if you fold the pants like this." She grabbed a pair of jeans to illustrate her method. Somehow, she folded, rolled, and tucked my pants into a small cylinder. "And for bonus points, when you unroll them, they won't have any wrinkles."

"Maya?" I asked her name gently because I gave zero care to if my pants got wrinkled. But she cared, and she'd made that clear in her organization of my entire house over the past month.

"Huh?" She'd already moved onto folding, rolling, and tucking another pair of pants.

"Do you want to pack for me?" I asked. "Because I would love your help."

She glanced up from the new pants cylinder, her eyes soft. "For real?"

"Do your thing, baby," I said, leaning in and giving her a kiss on the forehead. "Maybe it'll help with the clarity you're trying to find."

She melted into my touch. It didn't suck, that was for certain.

Honestly, I should've found a closet or a tool chest or something and really messed it up for her to fix. That's a thing she'd totally get off on.

"Like twenty more people reached out to me this morning about opportunities," she said, stepping away to go back to packing. "I don't even know where to begin to sort them out." She'd moved on to the boxer briefs. I couldn't describe how she did what she did to make them fit into a space two times smaller than what I figured they needed.

Even as she did her thing and made magic with my underwear, her anxiety oozed. I got it, the weight of all the contacts reaching out and pressing down on her. After the first dozen messages she'd shown me, it'd gotten overwhelming for me, too. And I wasn't the one corresponding with them.

"You need someone who knows the industry," I said.

Sure, I'd navigated the legalities of being a professional athlete, but I didn't do it alone. I made damn certain my team—even if they drove me nuts—had my best interests in play.

Maya frowned and tilted her head back to stare at the ceiling. "I sent some messages to friends and some of the headliners I've worked with. I just... It's hard to know who is really on my team, though? You know?"

"I know a guy," I said, certain I knew the perfect person to help solve this puzzle.

If there was one thing I'd learned, when you didn't fucking know what to do, you went to people who did. Then you listened to them and did what they said.

"All of these people know a guy, too." She pointed to the laptop with another pair of my boxers.

"But you don't know if you can trust them," I countered.

She blew out a defeated breath, even as she organized my suitcase in ways it'd never been organized before.

"You trust me?" I asked, already knowing the answer because a woman didn't let a man do the things we'd done that morning in the shower if she didn't have faith in his ability to take care of her.

"Of course, I trust you." She looked at me like I'd fumbled the ball right before hitting the end zone.

"Then when Elliott gets here, we're gonna loop him in," I said.

She frowned. "He reps sports athletes."

"But his connections never fail to surprise." There was a reason he'd been my agent for so long.

Maya trusted me. I trusted Elliott.

When Elliott arrived at our doorstep to drive my ass to training camp in Greeley, I knew I wasn't wrong about my choice to trust him with Maya. Elliott, in his spotless suit and with the confidence of only someone who knew how to wrangle the sharks in a cutthroat industry, would know which offer was best.

I may have made his life hard as hell with some of my previous mistakes, but Elliott was the best at fixing shit that I broke.

Here, since I hadn't broken anything yet, I figured his job would be cake. Maya laid it all out for him with a list of everyone who had cold-contacted her.

"There are messages and offers and more than a few inappropriate propositions," she said the last part with a frown.

Nope, I didn't like that frown or the propositions.

"I wish the answer was easy," she continued. "But I don't know these people, and the people I know are all recommending different things. I mean, this is my career, and I've finally got a shot. I can't wreck it right from the start."

"There's a dude in Denver," Elliott said after he finished scanning the list. "Owns a bar, and he's a big deal in the music industry. He's the one you need to talk to. I'll call a meeting."

"You trust him?" I asked, wanting that confirmation before anyone went near Maya's career.

"He's the one to trust," Elliott assured. "Let me make some calls, and I'll be there for the initial talk if that'd make you more comfortable."

"You'd do that for me?" Maya asked with a note of shock.

"Maya, you're my sister's friend, and you're Sloan's wife." He paused, seemed to make sure she heard every word he said because they were important. "And I consider you a friend, too. Of course, I'd do that for you. Honestly, I'm happy you're asking."

There was no escaping training camp, but Brek Montgomery—Elliott's contact—couldn't do the meeting straight away, anyway.

Maya's videos continued to skyrocket in the meantime, and Elliott kept mentioning how her value was only growing with each viral push. By the time we all gathered to meet at the dive bar Brek owned, Maya's value in the music industry had increased substantially.

Brek's Bar was a hidden gem tucked away in the corner of Denver. People in the city knew about the bar because Brek's connections with the music industry meant his performers were A-list. The guy had managed Dimefront for fuck's sake. He'd left his management role to run the bar when he met and fell in love with his wife. But Elliott was right, his connections with the industry were solid.

Brek brought along Hans—the current manager for Dimefront and pop sensation Sami Jo—to the meeting.

"You're the musician I keep hearing about," Hans said, holding his hand to Maya.

She shook it. "I mean…"

"Yes, she is," Elliott said with an air of authority that I really appreciated. "Her videos are currently trending on all major social media platforms. And without even trying, one of her homemade singles is trending on the two biggest streaming apps. Imagine what she could do with a professional studio and management."

He proceeded to lay out statistics I didn't even know existed about who was viewing, liking, and sharing Maya's reels. While Elliott detailed the stats, I leaned back in my chair like I was lounging and this wasn't a big deal, but I'd discreetly placed my hand on her back in a gesture of solidarity.

Not obvious so anyone else would even see, just so she'd know I was there and watching out for her.

"Look, I work with athletes," Elliott finished up after laying it all out. "Maya needs someone she can trust, and she's got so many offers that it's impossible to sift through them all in one sitting. Or four." He paused. Was he thinking, or was this for dramatic effect? "We came here because Brek knows the best. And Maya deserves the best. Is that you?"

"It's me, and I agree. Here's the deal. Dimefront goes on tour in three weeks," Hans said, looking only at Maya. "Sami Jo was their opening act, but she's now unable to perform."

Sami Jo was married to the Dimefront drummer, and she was a pop star in her own right. She'd had a breakout song about mozzarella sticks as a teenager, avoided all media for ages, and then broke back onto the scene when she and the Dimefront drummer connected. She was a big fucking deal.

"Sam will still be on tour with us, but not in a professional capacity," Hans added in that way managers do when they don't want to share too much information about a client, but you know the intel they've got is probably gossip worthy.

"Sam's pregnant, and she's taking it easy," Brek said, his hands folded behind his head. "Just tell her, Hans; she'll see for herself soon enough."

Hans gave Brek a look like he wasn't pleased with the interruption. "We've put feelers out for a replacement act, and given your popularity, I think you should take the job."

"You're offering to head my management team?" Maya asked, before Hans could say anything else. "Because I have some terms of my own that I'd like to bring into the mix."

Elliott looked at her like she'd lost her mind. But I had faith.

"I may be considered an overnight sensation, but I assure you

I've been doing this long enough to know what I'd like in representation." Now, it was her turn to lean in and take control of the meeting.

Hans sat up a touch straighter.

Brek seemed to enjoy this turn of events, what with his shit-eating grin.

"I don't want to agree to something like a tour without understanding how it fits into the entire fabric of my career. Too many times, artists are a one-and-done because they don't have a long-term plan." She didn't even blink as she continued, "I am not a one-and-done."

"No, no, you're not." Hans steepled his index fingers under his chin. "I've got some ideas for you. I think you'll like them, but launching with Dimefront is not a bad way to kick off your solo career."

"I know. It's likely the best way. I just want to ensure that I'm not only filler. That we're working toward the same goal," Maya said.

"I'll make some calls to my record label guys. With Hans on board, they'll take good care of you," Brek said. "Let's see if we can get the gears rolling on that before the tour starts."

Elliott lifted an eyebrow, but his wry smile gave him away.

"This sounds... this sounds perfect," Maya said, sliding her gaze to meet mine.

I might've been grinning like an idiot, but damn, I was proud of my wife.

CHAPTER
EIGHTEEN

MAYA

Given the abundance of animals out in the world, the insistence from his management that Sloan please not say anything that could be twisted, and my resistance to being ambushed in public, I hadn't spent a lot of time outside the house lately.

But tonight was Sloan's first pre-season game as a married man at Stallion Stadium. Of course, I was attending.

Angela even flew in for the game. Seeing as Angela wasn't a football fan, I was pretty sure she was only there to check on me.

That was nice, though, because I'd be checking on her, too, if the situation was reversed.

I'd arrived early with Sloan and hung out with Angela and Elliott until the game started. That was something I never actually thought would happen. Willingly hanging out with Elliott, I mean. But he wasn't the same as he used to be. He was actually down to earth, and well, I owed him for helping me out with the management sitch.

He finagled it so Angela and I didn't even have to sit in the stands, nabbing us an invitation to stay with some of the team's significant others in their special suite high above the field. The suite was air-conditioned, had private bathrooms, and a freaking phenomenal view. The signed jerseys and signed faded photos from past seasons were a very nice touch and added a nice ambiance.

I approved.

The best part of the suite was the small buffet table at the back with the usual game day snacks you'd expect at a stadium: popcorn and hot dogs with soda and beer. I brought my own ZipZing because those things were fire. I might have an addiction to them, but I was okay with it.

"Girl, you are here, and I cannot even handle how you're breaking the internet on the daily," Nisha gushed as she slid beside me, linking her arm with mine. She was clearly taking me under her wing. Which, let's be honest, I needed.

"I'm so glad to see you." I leaned into Nisha's arm, grateful for her support, and made the introductions with Angela.

"Why do you look like you're lost?" Nisha asked me with a warm smile. "These are your people. I promise you that. We're all in this together."

"Can I tell you a secret?" I asked.

"You better, now that you started with it." Nisha tilted her head to the side a smidge.

"This is my first pro game," I said, under my breath.

Nisha's eyes widened, clearly surprised.

"Me, too," Angela said, grimacing. "It's not really my thing."

"I've never even watched on TV," I said.

Nisha whispered, "Like ever?"

"The last football game I went to was soccer," I said quietly.

"Maybe let's not broadcast that part to the other plus-ones?" Nisha mimed zipping her lips.

Angela and I had seen Elliott play when we were all in high school together, but back then, he was less helpful and way more self-absorbed. Thanks to his attitude, he made sure any teenage infatuation I might've had with football players vanished. Pretty sure he handled that for Angela, too.

"Don't worry, I've got your back here." Nisha gestured to the end zone. "Okay, you see those pokey things at the end of the field? Those are called goal posts."

Angela and I laughed. Then I disentangled my arm so I could snag some popcorn. "I understand the basics. I've just never... been to a game."

"Not since high school," Angela added.

"Then welcome to your new home away from home," Nisha said, gesturing to the field.

I paused, tossing the popcorn in my mouth to study Sloan warming up on the field. He moved his tall frame with purpose, stretching and then jogging a quick sprint.

"I think this is one of my favorite parts of the game," Angela said, scanning the guys on the field.

"Me, too," Nisha said dreamily, as Darius did a toe touch stretch that put his backside on display.

"You're Maya Mitchell." One of the other women approached us. I hadn't met her before and was nearly certain she hadn't been at the Sloan Got Married to a Real Person Party.

I turned to her. "I am. Hi."

"I've seen your videos," the woman said with a huge smile. "Big fan."

"This is the new Shelby," another of the women said, stepping forward with a mini hot dog on her plate and a toothy smile.

"Who is Shelby?" Angela asked.

I wasn't entirely certain I wanted to know who that was since I was the new her.

"That's Ryan's ex-wife. They got a divorce, so she had to give up her seat in the box," Nisha said with a frown. "We're gonna miss her."

"But now we've got you," the first woman said. "I'm Denice, and this is Karie."

I actually felt bad for Shelby that she'd be missing the popcorn and...well...her friends.

"The new girls rarely stick around for long. It's very hard to be together with an athlete long term," Nisha said, letting that hang there in the air between us.

I waited for her to finish and tell me why it was hard to be with an athlete for the long term, but she didn't add to the statement.

"Because they're athletic?" I asked, going for a guess.

I had three sets of owl eyes blinking at me.

Nisha answered for them. "The guys travel all the time when they're on the team, and then when they retire, they either open a bunch of car dealerships and spend all their time there, or worse, they'll travel again with the broadcasting team."

"Or, even worse, they don't know what to do and just hang out at home all day," Denice added. "That's really the worst-case scenario."

"I want to hear all about your excitement," Nisha said. "How does it feel to be in everyone's ears?"

"It's kind of thrilling, actually." I tucked a piece of hair behind my ear. "And I got my first big break... I'm going to be opening for Dimefront on their upcoming tour."

Karie frowned, and Denice actually groaned.

"What?" My heart sank, because they were all being so nice. I figured they'd be happy for me.

"You'll do so great. Good luck with your future," Denice said as she and Karie patted my arm and headed for their seats.

"Why did that sound ominous?" Angela asked.

"Because, honey, they don't think Maya's going to last." Nisha pursed her lips. "But they like you, so that's a plus."

"Why don't they think I'm going to last?" I was genuinely curious. I mean, Sloan and I were going strong, and I was here supporting him.

"You're a performer, and you're already moving up the ranks as an artist." Nisha counted on her fingers. "This is Sloan we're talking about, and he might not be back next season." That was number two, then she counted the third finger—"And the two of you have a super couple name. Usually, anyone who ticks any of those boxes doesn't return for a repeat. But then you just added number four, and you're going to be traveling, and he's going to be traveling, and"—she draped her arm around my shoulders —"they've seen it happen before. It's hard to get close to someone and then have them break up."

"Sloan and I aren't breaking up," I assured. I actually considered explaining our situation and how we continued to slash expectations by working through them with salt and pepper shakers. I decided against it since it probably wouldn't make sense to anyone but us.

Pinpointing Sloan's location on the field wasn't hard at all. Funny, I had sampled those muscles the night before, so I knew what he tasted like. And yet the sight of him down there on the field, looking like a snack, made me want to lick him all over again.

I swear at that moment, he looked up in my direction. I nearly waved, but there was no way he could see me this far away, so instead, I just watched him toss a ball.

My hands got clammy as an intense desire to put my hands on Sloan, touch him, ensure we were okay, took hold.

Deep breaths.

"Don't worry about what they think," Angela assured. "They haven't seen you two together."

"I think you have a solid shot at staying in the game as the new Shelby," Nisha added.

My brain got all jumbled thinking about the nonsensical pieces of my life. I should try what Emily did, saying the first thing that came to mind.

"I do things all awkward. All out of order," I said, not really expecting that to be the first thing out of my mouth. "Which is why I've had multiple marriages that don't even count, but now, I have Sloan."

Maybe I should just go sit down? But then again, getting all of this out of my head made me feel lighter. Like gravity wasn't so intense right here in that stadium.

"Everything you've done to get to this point in your life has made you who you are," Angela said, totally serious. "We get stuck and think we're spinning our wheels. I get that. But just because you can't see the progress doesn't mean it's not happening."

"Your friend is smart. Listen to her," Nisha said.

I nodded and settled into my seat between Angela and Nisha. I couldn't tear my eyes away from Sloan. He moved with a graceful strength as he finished warming up, each stretch and jump a display of power and control. The muscles in his arms rippled as he tossed the ball back and forth with his teammates, his focus unwavering.

"The thing is, I want to keep him. We're happy. I enjoy being married to him," I said.

Nisha nodded as I spoke.

"A crappy day doesn't really matter because I wake up with him."

Angela squeezed my hand. "That's what matters. That's what moves you forward."

Nisha's eyes went soft, and she pulled her lips to the side. "Well, I don't know the future, but girlfriend, I'm sold."

Good. So was I.

As the national anthem filled the stadium, goosebumps prickled my skin. The crowd went silent, a collective hush falling over Stallion Stadium.

And then, with a roar that shook the foundations of the building, the game began.

My heart swelled with pride as I watched Sloan on the field, his every movement a testament to his passion for the game.

Beside me, Nisha let out a gasp of excitement as our team scored on the very first drive, the crowd erupting into cheers. Honestly, the energy in the suite was electric. That's how I got caught up in the thrill of it all, cheering alongside Nisha and the others.

It didn't matter that I was the new Shelby, and they didn't think Sloan and I would make it. Because I knew we'd be just fine. Which was excellent, because the camaraderie among all of us became palpable, a shared sense of pride and support binding us together.

I'd been wrong all this time. The excitement and the thrill were football. The game had nothing to do with Elliott and his volatile teenage hormones.

I'd been missing out, but that stopped right then.

CHAPTER
NINETEEN

SLOAN

Pre-season went better than expected, and the Stallions were favored going into the regular season.

Today, the late-afternoon sun slipped through the windows, casting a glow on the entire living room where Maya curled up in my arms, staring at the view. Even with everything that was wrong—I had to leave today for the first away game—everything felt right because we were together.

For now, at least.

My regular season was starting, which meant my time would be spent with the team, and she was heading out to rehearsals for the Dimefront tour, so her time would be there. We'd done the math, crunched the calendars, and we couldn't reconnect until the Dimefront opening night in Los Angeles.

That was weeks away. Weeks I was certain would feel like forever. But neither of us had mentioned the separation coming. The unspoken topic was off-limits.

We talked about everything else, but we didn't tackle the big issue. Instead, we made out on the couch and stared out the window together. She pressed a kiss to my mouth, and it heated in the familiar way because there was no lack of chemistry between the two of us.

"Maya," I whispered, brushing a lock of hair out of her eyes. "You know what's better than sitting here looking at the view?"

Her eyes twinkled. "I have some thoughts, but I'm curious about what you'll go with."

"Being outside in it." I waggled my eyebrows.

She frowned.

"C'mon, let's go for a hike," I said. "A little adventure before we have to... leave."

She scowled, but her heart wasn't in it. "No, I'm good inside. I like inside."

"I know you like inside, but you never go outside," I murmured, but her mouth was on mine, so it wasn't easy to get the words out.

Then she did the thing with her hand on my chest that was definitively her way of initiating sex. A totally unfair defense against my suggestion.

"I want to take you to my special spot," I murmured, trying to distract her from her absolutely unfair tactics.

"Mmm, I think I know your special spot."

My attempt to distract her didn't work, because then she was full on kissing me and climbing to straddle my lap with a mischievous glint in her eye.

"Please?" I asked, kissing her back because there was no way I wouldn't.

She sighed and pouted, while still straddling me as if staking her claim. "Sloan, there are bugs out there. I don't like critters."

I held her tighter, trying to reassure her with my touch. "I'll be there the whole time."

After a moment of silence, she finally said, "You won't let me out of this, will you?"

"Not a chance." I raised my right hand like a Boy Scout. "But I promise to protect you from all critters, big and small. I'll unleash my mighty roar and scare them off if they even think about approaching you."

She had to try not to laugh, but she failed.

"Fine. Get your superhero moves ready, bud." She dismounted from my lap and headed for her shoes.

While I missed the warmth of her body against mine, I did a fist pump because I would show her how amazing it could be up here in the mountains. It wasn't sunrise, but sunset could be pretty epic.

We stepped outside in the crisp air. The sky along the ridge was already turning to hues of pink and orange as the sun thought about setting.

Moving past the trash cans in the yard, I quickly stepped in front of her, taking a protective stance.

"What are you doing, you goof?" she asked while I blocked her path with my body.

"Protecting you from the bear you saw out the window that time."

"Har," she said. But her eyes glittered, and this thing we had between us was pretty fucking awesome.

Then I linked her hand with mine and pressed a kiss to her knuckles. "No worries. It's just a trash can. You're safe."

"You're a comedian," she said dryly.

I nodded. "Maybe that's what I'll do after I retire."

This was the last year on my contract, and I hoped I'd get renewed, but it was never too early to think about what came next.

"Perhaps come up with a backup plan to comedy?" She winked at me as I led the way into the trees. "Just in case."

"Now, who's the comedian?" I asked.

We stepped under the canopy of trees and the peace of the mountain fell on us in a kind of silence that wasn't awkward or unwelcome. This was the quiet I loved best. The simplicity of the leaves rustling and the brush of the soles of our shoes against the dirt.

"What is this place you're taking me to?" She kept up with my stride, coming beside me as the trail widened.

"Just a spot, really. I used to come here all the time as a kid." I pushed aside a branch so we could both go through, the rough bark scratching against my palm. "It's where Dad and I hiked since it's not too far, but far enough I felt like we'd gone somewhere."

"That's a metaphor for something, I'm sure of it," she said.

We continued on until a rustling in the underbrush made her pause and grip my arm with zero regard for her fingernails.

I reached for her hand gripping my biceps, and squeezed in reassurance, but she totally ducked behind me like she'd seen a trash can. The quiet sounds of nature suddenly seemed a helluva lot louder as a twig snapped and I actually jumped, too.

"We should go home," she whispered the words, but she didn't move.

The hit of her adrenaline meant that I was all on edge, too. But I'd walked this trail hundreds of times and saw nothing more dangerous than a bull snake.

Probably best not to mention the snake part to Maya because, with her rapid breathing and the way her body was all tensed up, she was freaking the fuck out, and it was rubbing off on me.

I practically expected to see a pair of gleaming eyes through the underbrush instead of the chipmunk that skittered out to run along the edge of the trail.

"Ladies love chipmunks," I said, mimicking Darius.

"What do you know about what ladies love?" she asked wryly.

"I think we're going to be all right," I assured, removing her hand from my arm because she was seriously going to leave a bruise.

She pulled her lips to the side. "That was a chipmunk."

"Yeah," I said. "And if you're lucky, you might even see a hawk or an owl."

I didn't mention the snakes. Honest to goodness, I didn't see one that often.

"You may not give me any shit about that." Maya pointed to where the chipmunk had emerged.

I pasted on my best imitation of innocence. "I would never."

We both knew that I absolutely would—and often.

"Pfft," she said.

Now, it was my turn to squeeze her shoulder. "You've got to admit that it's nice out here."

She stared at where the chipmunk had disappeared. "I'll admit that I have yet to be attacked or bitten by anything," she agreed. "Which makes it nice out here."

"I'll take it," I said, jumping to high five one of the branches above.

We trekked on ahead, letting the trail lead the way, neither of us needing to add commentary to the beauty that was this mountain. The trail opened up to a meadow that would fill with wildflowers in the spring. Right now, it was mostly dry grass and pebbles, but it was still pretty. A different pretty.

I led her off to the west side to the big-ass boulder that came about up to my waist.

When I was a kid, though? Man, this rock felt like my personal mountain.

"Ta-da," I said, gesturing to the spot.

"It's a rock," she said with mock excitement.

Not gonna lie, I figured she'd have a different reaction. My disappointment must have showed, because she lifted her eyes to meet mine, and I saw a shift in her expression—from playful teasing to a deeper understanding.

"It's my rock," I said. "I've never brought anyone here before. This place was just for me and Dad. It's… special."

She nodded, touching the stone with reverence. "Then that makes it an amazing rock."

"It does, doesn't it?" I placed my hand on top of the boulder next to hers. "Years of visits up here. Some with Dad. Most just me. Now, this time with you."

"You know what's funny?" she asked, setting her hand on top of mine.

"Nope, but I'd love to find out." I turned my hand over to twine our fingers together.

"I enjoy being your wife, Sloan."

I swallowed the lump in my throat.

"All the times I've been married, and I've never had the full wife experience… until you," she continued with a squeeze of my hand. "No one has ever shown me their rock before."

"Well, I'm glad you're enjoying what we have. I enjoy being a husband, too." I toyed with the wedding ring on her finger.

"I kind of thought it'd be boring." She looked up at me, her eyes misty. "That we'd get sick of being in each other's space, but I'm seriously going to miss you."

"Maya." I cupped her face in my hands. "I'm going to miss you more."

We settled on the boulder, side by side, our gazes fixed on the horizon where the sun dipped lower. As the shadows lengthened and a cool breeze swept through the meadow, Maya leaned closer, burrowing into me.

One simple gesture, but with it, we seemed to hit our stride.

CHAPTER
TWENTY

MAYA

My heart raced with the soft hum of anticipation before the music started and the stage lights flooded the Puffle Yum Stadium in Los Angeles. I was finally there, under the spotlight by myself, showing the world that I didn't belong in the background. The stadium was packed with an enormous crowd, and the surge of electricity coursing through me made me feel unstoppable.

I started my set a cappella, in the darkness, followed by a smidge of guitar. And then the lights came up, the band joined in, and this was happening. I let the music guide my movements, embraced the glittered jumpsuit Hans' team—my team—suggested, and let it be my turn. The crowd was seriously into this and if I let it, this whole thing would definitely give me a god complex.

Angela and Emily showed up to support me on opening night. They would've come no matter what, but it didn't hurt that my invitation came with backstage Dimefront passes.

Sloan flew in, too. From the side of the stage, his gaze fixed on me with an intensity that sent shivers down my spine. And when the last note of my songs faded, and the spotlight clicked off, I stood breathless.

I blinked away the fleeting imprints the bright lights in the stadium left in my vision, and the dreamlike quality they added, before the crew whisked me off the stage.

Dimefront came out right behind me. Their lead singer, Bax, offered a high-five on his way past. And when the first chords of their new song hit, the crowd went bonkers again.

Backstage, hands reached out toward me, guiding me past the cords and boxes, curtains and people. Out the exit door, I headed for the meet-and-greet tent with Sloan right behind me. I turned my head to confirm, and despite the distractions and the clamor all around us, his gaze met mine for a moment. The unspoken conversation between us transcended the noise and the excitement.

He mouthed, "You were amazing."

My heart swelled at the compliment.

"Angela and Emily aren't coming out, yet," I said to him. "They wanted to see the Dimefront guys."

The junket, with a few press and a handful of influencers for interviews, wouldn't be nearly as much fun for them.

Moving from the darkness of backstage to the bright sunlight, I squinted as I made my way past the line of waist-high metal fencing that blocked the area between the stage and the tent. Fans along one edge of the fence clamored for autographs and selfies. Hans had told me this would happen. He'd also told me to hoof it to the tent, wave, and smile, but nothing more, because there wasn't time for me to pause.

As much as I wanted to stop, sign things, and say hello, I followed Hans' instructions and kept going.

"Maya," one guy near the front of the fence shouted so loud, I couldn't help but turn his way.

He humped the air as he continued to yell my name. "Maya! Come have a go!"

The lewd motion definitely caught my attention and made bile rise in my throat.

Sloan yelled back to the man, "Back the fuck off and show some respect!"

The guy tried to jump into the fenced area, but he couldn't get his leg over the metal rail. Even if he had succeeded, two security guards were already there, pushing him back over to his side.

The thing was that I was safe. Sloan was at my back, and a security guard was at my side.

That guy couldn't get to me. I tucked my chin and motored forward, head down.

"Fine. Keep walking, bitch!" the man shouted, and he spat in my direction. It full on sounded like he'd hocked a loogie.

When somebody called a person a bitch, or they spat phlegm in their direction, the tendency was to stop and reassess the situation. Which was what I did—I stopped short.

"Keep going." The security guard at my side shuffled me forward and, okay, I had a lot of emotions about this. But security dude was correct; now wasn't the time. I gulped and committed to hustling to the tent when it seemed to get colder behind me.

I turned to confirm Sloan was still there, but my pulse kicked up because he wasn't.

He stalked toward the guy with his fists balled, his chin jutted, and a general fierceness that made me worry he'd end up in prison if he kept that direction.

"Sloan," I called, but he didn't seem to hear me.

I started back toward him, but the security guy shook his head. "No. We keep moving."

I did not, in fact, keep moving. But I didn't follow Sloan, either.

"You have something to say?" Sloan asked, stalking toward Mr. Hump-the-Fence.

My heart was racing, and this wasn't how I wanted to end my first time on an actual stage as a solo artist.

The guy seemed to shrink back from the bulk that was Sloan towering over him.

"I asked if you have something to say," Sloan said, not getting in the guy's face but definitely too close for my comfort. Close enough to take a swing if he wanted to.

"No." The guy shook his head. "Nothing to s-s-say."

He seemed terrified, and well, so was I.

And not because there were paparazzi and cameras everywhere, but Sloan looked like a man ready to fight for my honor. To be clear, no one needed to be injured on behalf of my honor. This was the twenty-first century, and my honor was just fine, even if some guy humped the air when I walked by.

"Sloan!" I called as loud as I could. So loud, my voice cracked.

After the performance and the overall excitement, screaming his name like that didn't feel great.

"No one messes with what's mine," Sloan said to the guy, low and deep and serious as hell. "We clear?"

The heckler had turned a strange shade of gray, but he nodded all the same.

Honestly, I think everyone in the vicinity nodded. Sloan was that serious.

Sloan nodded and smiled huge like this was Finn or Darius, and they were just shooting the shit. "Good. That woman is my wife. You see her ever again? You do not look at her. You do not talk to her. You turn and go the other way. You get me?"

The other guy nodded again, and honestly, I felt a bit gray myself.

Sloan started to walk back to me, but he stopped. Turned on his heel and said, "You ever have the chance to be in the presence of beauty like hers again? You show some goddamned respect."

I didn't know about everyone else, but I gulped. Hard.

Sloan said nothing else as he took his place behind me again. His slow gait and nonchalance made it seem as though nothing had happened.

"You need more security," he said, simply.

We were still in public, and I was riding on so many feelings all in a short period, I needed a second to process.

I waited until we got to the big, white, circus-style event tent. I pulled my husband aside, sighed, and said, "Sloan... what the hell was that?"

"That was a fucker who needed to be set straight," Sloan responded.

He didn't seem to understand why I might get distressed at his choice to approach said fucker.

"Security had it handled," I said, crossing my arms.

"I helped them," he replied. "The dude threatened you. That doesn't happen on my watch."

"This isn't your watch," I countered. "This is my job."

He didn't reply to that.

"And now, you've made a scene. Now, when I go into these interviews, what I say doesn't even matter because everyone is going to be talking about you and...and...Sir Humps-a-Lot!"

His expression faltered, and he was genuinely thinking about what I'd said.

"If I don't get to stop and sign autographs, you don't get to stop and play security," I said with a huff.

"Okay," he said.

"That's it?" I asked.

"Yeah."

"That might be my least favorite response of all the responses," I said.

"What happened out there? I get it. It shouldn't have happened," Sloan admitted, staring at the asphalt floor. "None of it. The guy being so close to you, me confronting him, or you feeling like you got upstaged at your own event."

He looked up at me with those damn puppy eyes, and the good dose of mad I'd been nursing disintegrated.

"We're married, but we're equals in this relationship. And people like that are going to be everywhere," I said, stepping into his space and dropping my forehead against his chest.

He pulled me against him. "But he was here, and I was here, and I didn't think. I just acted. I'm sorry about that."

"It would be so much easier to stay angry at you if you'd argue with me about this." I stepped back because I had interviews to get to.

He pulled his lips between his teeth. "The media loves me when they get a whiff of a scandal. This won't go in my favor. We both know that."

"Since we're a team, it won't get edited in my favor either," I said, deflated.

"I am sorry," he apologized once more. "I promise not to do that again."

I nodded and headed back to my team. Hans stood there, and he didn't look pleased, but he rarely looked pleased, so that wasn't anything new.

"Maya," Sloan called my name.

I turned back to him.

"Are we good?" he asked.

I nodded. "We're good."

———

SLOAN

After all was done, and I was headed back to Denver, Elliott made sure I understood no one was happy about this turn of events. The Stallions weren't pleased about the photos—that looked a fuckuva lot worse than they should've—of me tearing Maya's "fan" a new asshole. A couple of new endorsement deals were now on the fritz. Elliott was pissed that he would have to smooth things over. Again.

Maya deserved someone more levelheaded than I'd been, and I promised to be that man.

The cherry on top of the shit sundae was that I was getting chewed the fuck out again, and I wished it was Maya doing the chewing because at least she was fun to look at while she laid into me.

"You aren't security," Coach yelled, throwing his clipboard on the desk and shoving his hands on his hips. "What the fuck were you thinking?"

"I wasn't," I answered. "I wasn't thinking."

After I got off the plane, my escort took me straight to his office in Denver so he could let me know how badly I'd screwed up.

"You want some jackass to come on the field and play your position for you?" Coach was getting red in the face, but even I knew he was only getting started.

I knew better than to say anything, so I just shook my head to answer his question.

"No. You don't want that," he said, pacing the room. "Because you're a professional, and that's your job. But now, you're a security guy? You can just hop into any situation where there's a need for security and handle it all by yourself?"

He paused, and I guessed now, it was my turn to respond. Which was good because I was ready for this to be over.

"Coach." I held up my hands. "I didn't know there was enough security. I was worried. I got scared he'd get to Maya. He spat at her, and I lost my cool. I didn't handle the situation the way you or Maya would've liked. For that, I'm sorry."

All the heated anger seemed to get sucked out of the room.

"There's no attitude?" Coach asked, more than a little deflated.

"Nah." I shook my head. "I'm genuinely sorry that I caused trouble for Maya and trouble for the team. Maya and I worked it out, and I hope you know this won't happen again. If I gotta run sprints, I'll do it. You wanna give me a fine and suspend me from the next game? It'll suck, and I think it's the wrong call, but I get that it's not my call to make. Whatever you decide, I understand. No hard feelings from me."

That brought Coach up short.

"No attitude at all?" Coach asked, disappointed that he didn't get to continue reading me the riot act.

"Promise," I assured. "Look, I'm not sorry for what I said to the guy. But I know I made an unpleasant situation worse with how I handled it. Next time, I'll let the professionals deal with it."

"Well..." Coach obviously didn't know what to do with me.

"We good?" I asked the same question I'd given Maya.

Coach nodded, squinting at me like he didn't believe what he was seeing. "We're good."

Hands in my pockets, head down, I started to walk away, but Coach cleared his throat. "You showed more restraint than I would've if he'd spat at my wife."

I nodded. "Well, then we both have shit to work on."

"I guess we do," he said.

"Is that a smile? 'Cause it looks like you're smiling, and the coach I know doesn't smile when he's letting me have it." I shrugged.

"Yeah, well, I guess we both have shit to work on," Coach said, gruff as fuck, before going back to his mess of a desk.

"Hey, Sloan?" he asked.

"Yeah?"

"I'm proud of you," he said, holding my gaze with his.

I would never admit this to anyone, but my throat got all clogged up at his words, and I had to choke back the emotion that had no business in a locker room.

CHAPTER
TWENTY-ONE

MAYA

Our schedules didn't line up, at all and when Sloan was available to talk, I was on stage or getting ready to go on stage or in the VIP tent doing a meet and greet. When I was available to talk, he was in practice, a game, or a post-game interview.

> Maya: I missed your call. I can tlk now?

> Sloan: heading 2 practice. Talk in a couple hours?

> Maya: Show prep then. Sry

> Sloan: I miss you

> Maya: Miss u 2

———

> Sloan: your voicemail made my night.

Maya: I swear soon we'll catch a break and get to tlk

Sloan: I miss you

Maya: miss u 2

———

Maya: Heading to bed. I'm spent.

Sloan: ...

Maya: I'll call tmrw

Sloan: 'night

———

Sloan: Good flight. Just landed in Miami

Maya: Headed 2 show rt now

Sloan: break a leg

Maya: Play hard. Don't break anything.

And that was the general gist of how it went for us.

But tonight, we'd sorted our schedules and since we were in the same time zone, he would skip the post-game interview and I'd skip dinner.

My phone rang right as I hit the door to my hotel room.

"Sloan," I said his name into the phone as I flipped the latch on the door and leaned against it.

The Dimefront guys all traveled with their families, so they insisted on comfort, and that meant only the best hotels.

"Maya," he said my name like he was lost at sea, and my voice was there to rescue him.

I got that because, damn, was I relieved, too.

I dropped my bag on the chair near the window and flopped onto the mattress. I'd changed out of the rhinestones at the stadium and into sweatpants and a cropped tank top.

"Tell me about everything," he said, his voice low and comforting—and, gah, just listening to him made me want to quit everything, jump on a plane, and then jump on him.

"Every day is different, and every day is the same," I said, turning to my side to prop the phone against my ear. "But tonight's show was so good. The band was on fire, and the audience was just in it."

"Yeah?" he asked, clearly waiting for me to say more.

"You want to video call?" I asked, already pushing the button to turn the audio into a video.

Sloan's face was on the screen, and my heart was finally happy, until the buffering wheel of doom spun and the damn call dropped.

"No, no, no." I started to call him back, but my phone was already ringing.

"Hi," I said. "The call—"

"Maybe we stick to this right now?" he asked with a chuckle. "I don't want to lose you again tonight."

"How was practice?" I asked, putting the phone on speaker and settling in so I wouldn't touch anything else that might disconnect us.

Sloan told me all about the team, about the hotel where he was staying, and all about how Elliott had gotten him a meeting with the ZipZing people again.

Sloan was, as expected, not so keen on the idea, given the history.

And then there was a rustling of his bedding, the muffled noise of him moving on the mattress.

"Are you in bed?" I asked, already knowing the answer.

"Yeah, you?" he asked.

"I am," I said. "I don't want to get up for a full twenty-four hours. I swear I could just sleep. But then I try to sleep, and I toss and turn."

"Same," he said. "Fuck, I miss you."

"What are you doing now?" I asked, squirming a little because hearing his voice had caused an ache between my thighs.

"Pretty sure I'm about to put my hand on my dick and ask you to tell me a story," he said.

Well, that sounded like a fine time to me, too. I could curse the buffering wheel of doom and poor Wi-Fi, but there was something to be said for just hearing him talk to me that way.

Now, my body was all buzzing with energy, and I had that vision of him with his hand on himself and his face going slack and—

"I mean, since sleep isn't likely," he said, uncertain.

"And we're married. Alone. And I'd love to help you…uh…get a handle on things?" I agreed. "I think right now, we have to do whatever we can do to get through this separation."

There was more rustling on his end, and I'd never actually done this before, like this, so I didn't have any experience to go on.

"How…uh…how does this work?" I asked.

Obviously, I understood the logistics, but did we lay ground rules or expectations? Should I get the salt and pepper?

"Well, gorgeous, I suppose you put your hand between your legs and do whatever you do to get yourself there. And I'd do my thing on this end."

Okay, sure, well, I got that part.

"Sloan," I said, a little uncertain that I'd even be good at this.

"Maya," he said my name in a way that gave me a total hit of confidence.

It'll work! It'll work!

"You think an...um...a...release...will help you sleep?" I asked.

"Yes," he said, simply. "It almost always works for me."

Oh.

I said nothing because what was I supposed to say?

"Do you, uh, do it a lot?" I asked. I mean, I was his wife, so it was fine for me to ask the question.

"Handle things while you're away?" He chuckled, low and deep. "Only if I want to sleep."

I made a garbled noise, because now I had to think about the fact that when he texted me g'night, and we weren't able to connect, I'd be going on stage or something like that, and he'd be "handling" things.

"Maya?" he asked.

"Hmmm?"

"You want to do this?"

"Sure." That came out way too perky and not so enthusiastic. Shit. "I mean"—I took a deep breath—"yes, I want to do this with you."

"Move your hand under your pajamas, Maya. Between your legs," he said, and the command in his voice? Oh, yes, please!

"Tell me what you feel," he asked, his voice rough and gravelly.

Damn, damn, damn. I slipped under the blankets because I couldn't just do this right on top of them.

"Maya," he said my name as a command. "Hand between your legs, baby."

I did as I was told, moving my hand underneath the duvet, beneath the drawstring band of my pajama bottoms, down between my legs, to the spot I knew intuitively would make me—

Yup, I moaned.

"What do you feel, gorgeous?" he asked.

"I'm wet for you." I was. So soaked. I circled the bundle of nerves above my opening and bit at my lip to stop myself from moaning.

A vision of him over the top of me was right there in my

periphery, his hard length filling me, his breath against my cheek, his beard brushing my jaw.

"Sloan," I murmured. To be honest, I wasn't entirely certain which Sloan I spoke to—vision Sloan or reality Sloan. It didn't matter though. My body was primed for both of us, and I was the only one here.

"I want to be inside you," real Sloan said over the line. "I see your picture and get your texts, and all I want is to taste you and feel your legs wrapped around my shoulders."

I pressed harder against the bundle of nerves at the apex of my thighs. Circling the wetness there and letting the sensations carry me away.

"I want you, too," I said, lifting my hips for better pressure.

He wasn't even there in the same room, and the energy between us still sizzled and snapped. This wasn't sexual tension. This was straight-up desire.

"Use two fingers and take care of things for me," he said, his words low and husky. "My hands are full."

"Sloan, are you..." Getting off on this? Relaxing? Enjoying things? Going to sleep? Dabbling in a touch of embroidery while I—

"Focus on yourself," he said. Again, like it was a command.

I was Maya, and this was insanely hot, but I didn't have to take orders from anyone, thank you.

"Maya," he said with that bedroom tone of his.

Actually, I didn't mind taking orders from him. Not like this, anyway.

Whatever, they were good orders, so who was I to question them?

I circled myself again. Slipping a fingertip down to tease my entrance, I pressed against the warm spot inside that always got me there faster.

"Tell me what you're doing?" he said.

Uh... "Touching myself." As requested, commander.

I didn't say the last part.

"You rubbing your cherry?" he asked.

"Uh-huh," I said, as I hit a nice sensitive spot that made the sound breathy.

"Flick it," he commanded.

Um, 'scuse me?

"I said to flick it, Maya," he said, again. "Use your finger and do it."

Um... that wasn't...

"Maya," he said in a growl, and I totally flicked it.

And that's how my trek up Orgasm Mountain sped up. Huh, I was breathing hard, and my heels were on the mattress, my knees bent. I didn't even care that the blankets had fallen away, and I was wide open.

I moaned. I did. My hand circled and pressed and did things exactly right.

All I could think of was the way his tongue would feel against my nipple as his hand continued down between my legs...

"You're a very good girl, Maya," he said, his voice raspy.

I nearly came. Just from a little touch of Sloan praise and a flick I didn't even know would feel good.

"Slide your hand along your dick," I said, shifting against the sheets. Wishing he was there, and this was his finger and his hand and—

"Yes, baby." He made a noise that was sort of a grunt and sort of a purr, and he handled things.

I edged myself closer to climax with only that vision of him over the top of me.

"Squeeze yourself," I said. Then I cleared my throat and did my best to use an effective I-command-you-to-do-it tone. "Move your thumb up the indentation along the edge of the tip while you do it. Imagine it's my tongue there."

I kept onward up Big "O" Mountain, while he took care of his own mountain-climbing excursion.

The vision of Sloan in my mind was pure performance art.

I circled and pressed. He grunted and thrust into his hand.

149

My mouth went dry, and little stars danced behind my eyes even as the thread of our connection strung tight.

"Come for me," he said, and I didn't even know he was holding my orgasm hostage like that. But my body was waiting for his permission.

There wasn't a choice for me here, since my body took his command, and I finished right there, breathing hard and feeling like I'd just had him there with me. Inside me.

"Mine," he said as I moaned.

Then he made the low rumble of a growl he did when he came, and I could practically see his hot release splashing in streaks across his belly.

He grunted again, and I said, "Yours."

The thing was, I absolutely meant it.

We stayed on the phone breathing heavily, neither of us saying much.

"I think I'm actually tired," I said, finally.

"Maya," he said my name like some kind of plea. "We'll be together soon."

I adored that he said that, but I didn't believe him. I'd seen the schedules. I understood the reality.

CHAPTER
TWENTY-TWO

SLOAN

Maya's dressing room was lush. This wasn't a locker room tonight, for damn sure. Not with the buckets of flowers every-fucking-where and the racks of Maya's costumes.

This was where Hans had me wait when her show finished, and Dimefront took over as headliner.

She didn't know I was coming. Fuck, until that afternoon, *I* hadn't known I was coming.

But we had an extra twenty-four hours between practice and the next game. Coach told me to get the hell out of town, Elliott handed me a ticket to Seattle, and I didn't ask questions.

That was how I got there, standing in Maya's dressing room, waiting for my wife.

The second Maya saw me there, it only took her two-point-five seconds to realize I wasn't a mirage. She practically slammed the door behind her and ran straight to me.

Maya, in my arms, thank fuck, finally.

"You're here." She wrapped her arms around my neck and let me lift her as our mouths met. Her lips were hungry as my arms held tight around her body.

There was no way I was letting her go quickly. Damn, but I'd missed the feel of her body against mine.

"I'm here," I said, barely breaking away from her mouth before going back for more. At this rate, I'd kiss all the lipstick right off her lips.

We kept at it, letting the time and space we'd been apart fall between us to our feet. Because now we were together, sharing the same air, and there was nothing I wanted more.

"Did you get to see me?" she asked against my neck.

"You were amazing," I said, choking up a little and just letting that shit ride because I was here, and she was here, and even if it was a dressing room, I wasn't about to hide how I felt.

She pulled away just enough so our noses touched. "Really?"

"I'm so fucking proud of you," I said.

Still nose-to-nose, she smiled against my mouth. "I can't believe you're here."

"I told you we'd see each other soon."

"You kept your promise," she said.

For Maya, there was no question I kept my promises.

I tilted my head to the side a bit when I added, "Pretty sure Elliott was also tired of me complaining about missing you, so he put my ass on a plane."

We ignored the light knock on her dressing room door. We were exactly where we were supposed to be, and there was nobody else in the universe but the two of us.

Unfortunately, reality was behind that knock and while Dimefront played their show, Hans needed to go over recording times for Maya in the studio when the tour took a break.

Then we did the VIP meet-and-greet, ate dinner with the band, and finally, thank fuck, headed back to the hotel.

By the time we made it to her suite at The Four Seasons, I figured we wouldn't be able to keep our hands off of each other.

But that's not exactly how it went. Not when we had the entire night together, and we both wanted to savor every second. I wished I could slow time down, or that there was a way I could make it stop for just a little while.

So instead of kissing the hell out of her like I'd figured I would, I stepped close and wrapped my arms around her. Pulled her tight against me. Held her close and pressed my lips to the top of her head. Stopping to just feel everything that was her.

She allowed the moment, sank into me, and didn't rush, either.

We stood like that for a long time, before my body had enough of waiting and I lifted her chin with my fingertip, leaned in, and brushed my lips over hers.

We kissed long and deep, while my heart pounded in my chest and my hands worked the zipper at the back of her dress.

The only sound in the room was our breaths coming quicker and the metal-on-metal of the zipper lowering. Her skin was soft under my hands as she pulled her arms from the dress and let it fall to the floor.

I should've done something, touched her, but all I could do was stare at the woman. I'd seen her naked loads of times. Pretty sure I had a Ph.D. in studying her body with my tongue, for fuck's sake. But tonight, I truly took her in—the way her nipples puckered with desire and her perfect breasts hung heavy. The way her breaths came and went. The way the swell of her belly led to the triangle of trimmed curls underneath her pink panties.

I lifted my hand to her breast, holding it in my palm and brushing my thumb over the center of her nipple. She drew in a gasp, and I moved the other palm along the side of her stomach, down between her legs, and under the fabric to heaven.

She hitched one leg against my thigh to give me better purchase, and I took full advantage of the opportunity.

I used my fingers to make her wet, while my other hand continued to tease lightly against her breast.

I didn't kiss her, though. I just let the panting between us mingle in the air until her body asked for more, and she moved against my fingers, clenching and releasing around them.

153

God, but I was hard as steel, my dick practically begging to be inside her.

It wasn't me who made us stop. No, it was Maya who dismounted from my fingers and pushed me toward the bed. Well, I let her.

My shirt went first, then my pants and boxers, until the only thing between our bodies was a bit of oxygen and her silk panties. She handled the panties part before she was even on the bed with me.

I let her have control of what came next, while my dick pulsed in her hand, and her mouth moved down my chest. She dragged her lips over my skin so the soft, wet inside of her mouth trailed past my navel, along the trail of hair leading to—

Her mouth was on my dick, and her hand held my nuts, and fuck it all, being married was the best thing drunk—or sober—me had ever done.

She moved her mouth up and down my shaft, deep-throating and then releasing to start again. I'd have a lipstick ring when she was done, and damn, that made me even harder.

The wet heat of her pressed against my thigh while she went down on me, rubbing in circles. That she was getting off on that didn't hurt my feelings. But my nuts pulled up close to my body, and I was gonna blow if she kept this up.

"Gorgeous, if you don't want me to finish, then you should probably climb on," I said. There was only so much control I had, and we were quickly coming to the limit.

She didn't seem to care that I might finish, because she gave me two more thrusts into her mouth before she came up for air. I hissed a breath, because fuck, it was cold without the warmth of her mouth. Her tongue.

I started to sit up so I could take over, but she wasn't having it. She held my chest down with her hand as she mounted me, holding on while she slipped her body into place. Tight and wet, she enveloped my dick, and I couldn't stop myself from bucking under her.

Usually, I'd take this part slow, ease in, and let her body adjust to taking my heavy girth. But tonight, something came over me, and there was no pause button.

She didn't seem to care. Seemed to get off on it, even.

"That's it, baby," I said, holding her hips down and giving her my thumb against the bundle of nerves beneath the curls at the center of her thighs.

"Flick it," she said, pressing my finger right where she wanted it.

I did three soft taps, a swipe, and then flicked. And she came, pulsing around me, milking my shaft until there was nothing left.

Her eyes stayed open the whole time her body pulsed around me, her gaze locked with mine. The connection was something I'd never experienced before. Something different that felt so right.

Gently, I sat up, holding her against me and running my hand over the back of her hair. Then, with as much care as possible, I laid her down beside me and got up from the bed to run warm water on a washcloth.

Neither of us said anything as I cleaned between her legs.

We'd never done it like this before. She usually took charge and handled this part, but tonight was different. Special. She was a queen, and I was there to worship her, care for her, and... love her.

The thought took my breath away and made the world seem to go two-dimensional.

"God, I'm in love with you," I said, the words slipping out as easily as a moan or a groan or any of the other sounds we'd made together.

Maya stilled. She didn't move at all. It actually felt like she'd left the bed, even though she was right there with me.

"Sorry," I said, quickly, and tossed the washcloth aside. "I'm sorry. That just came out."

Maya sat up so we were face to face, her expression unreadable as her eyebrows drew together, and a slight frown marred what was otherwise a fucking fantastic time.

"We should go to sleep," I suggested, hastily, already climbing under the covers.

For the first time in our marriage, things traveled well past awkward down the road to totally fucked.

"Sloan..." She looked at me funny. I couldn't quite figure out that expression. I'd never seen it on her before.

"Are you tired?" I asked, stretching my arm out to settle her in the crook like we always slept when we were together.

She nodded. "I am."

"Then let's get some shut eye, yeah?" I asked, gesturing to my arm.

She forced a smile but settled in with me, her back to my front. We might've both been naked, but I was certain I was the only one who felt exposed.

There in the dark with the sounds of our breathing and the occasional rustle of blankets as she shifted, I'd never been so worried that I'd get kicked out of bed. Out of the room. Out of her life.

But then from the darkness, she said, "I'm so glad you're here, Sloan."

And she turned into my embrace to kiss me lightly on the mouth.

I kissed her back. "Get some sleep."

She smiled against my lips, and I hoped to hell that things might just be okay.

CHAPTER
TWENTY-THREE

MAYA

Sloan was here, and he held me loosely while he slept. Being the big spoon to my little spoon while his breaths gently whispered against my hair.

God, I'm in love with you... His words hung in the air, taunting me.

Um... so that had happened. I pulled my bottom lip between my teeth, while every muscle in my body seemed on edge.

I closed my eyes and tried to force myself to relax into Sloan's embrace.

I mean, I had him here with me. It was what I wanted. What I'd dreamed about for so many nights alone.

The weight of the soft duvet and Sloan's embrace should've grounded me. But as I lay there, lost in the haze of my fear, nothing felt right. With Sloan's words, the world went slightly out of focus. Not enough to throw me into total disarray, but enough that if I thought about it long enough, I'd get a headache.

And I couldn't stop thinking about it.

I opened my eyes, willing myself to sink deeper into the mattress and find solace in the safety of Sloan's presence.

God, I'm in love with you...

But, no, his words continued to play on repeat in my mind. A ridiculous loop that wouldn't allow me to drift into sleep.

There wasn't even anything for me to organize.

My body shook a little as I searched for calm that wouldn't come. Even if there was something to distract me, nothing would take my mind off the words that he'd said. Or worse, the way the truth was obvious in his eyes as he spoke them.

Gah, this wasn't what I'd signed up for in the marriage with Sloan.

He'd fallen in love with me.

And now that he'd said the words, he couldn't take them back.

Sure, he could apologize, but the play had already been called. Even if he could take them back, it didn't matter. This was how he felt, and that didn't change.

I tried to time my breaths with his, but where his were even, mine just came out shaky.

We said we wouldn't fall in love. That'd been the cornerstone of this marriage. The reason it could work.

We'd promised to keep love out of it.

CHAPTER
TWENTY-FOUR

SLOAN

I'd told her I was in love with her, and things went off center between us. The weight of my confession pulled us in different directions. I wasn't upset that I'd told Maya how I felt about her or how things had changed for me. Yeah, I was sorry as fuck that I'd just dropped the words like an explosive in the middle of our night together after the most amazing orgasm of my life.

There were so many ways I could've told her how I felt that would've made a helluva lot more sense.

That was fine, though. I'd said something that changed the foundation we'd built our marriage on. It would take time to adjust.

In her dressing area at the concert the next afternoon, Maya prepared to go onstage, and I got ready to head out to San Francisco for the next regular season game.

"I'll let you know when I land," I said to Maya.

She was in the makeup chair, focused on her reflection in the mirror, while the stylist scraped on a lot of black eyeliner.

"I'll be waiting," Maya said with a sad smile. Her voice stayed steady despite the lingering heaviness.

I texted Elliott to confirm that he'd be picking me up from the stadium to get my ass to the airport.

"Hans said I could cut the last song so I'll be able to see you off," she said, her eyes meeting mine in the mirror, reflecting a mix of emotions I couldn't quite decipher.

I should've felt guilty about her cutting the show short—but I didn't. The world got my wife most of the damn time, but this time, I got her.

With her makeup done, Maya stood up from the chair, ready to face the crowd waiting for her out in the arena. She was opening for Dimefront, but she was a superstar in her own right now.

She turned to me once more. This time, there was a softness in her eyes that made my heart ache.

"Hey," I said, pulling her toward me and hugging her carefully so I wouldn't jack with her lipstick. "I'm sorry about—"

She lifted her fingertips against my lips. "This is a salt and pepper discussion. Not a pre-show talk."

I nodded because she was right. She was just about to head on stage, and this wasn't where her mind needed to be.

"Then I'll see you when we're in Denver next?" I asked hopefully.

She shook her head. "We've got the press thing in New York and then the concert in Baltimore."

"I'm gonna be on the West Coast." With practice between away games.

"Hans can coordinate with Elliott?" she suggested. "The two of them can figure it out for us?"

"That's why we have managers, I guess." But I didn't like the idea of Elliott being in charge of my time-with-Maya schedule.

I also couldn't get across the country and back in time to make everyone happy. Not even myself.

"There's still FaceTime," Maya said, gently. "If we find ourselves with decent Wi-Fi."

"You know I'm your biggest fan, and there isn't one thing in the world that will change that?" I asked.

She nodded as she held her arms wide so one of the guys could attach her earpiece, and run it down the back of her rhinestones to the control box at her lower back.

"We're running about ten minutes late," a roadie said from the doorway. "Problem with an amp, but it's getting swapped out now."

"Do what we need to do. The show must go on," Maya said with a reassuring smile.

"I'll see you after?" she asked me as a blinged-out microphone was slipped into her palm, and the crew shuffled her to the wings of the stage.

"I hope so." But it wasn't looking promising. Even if she cut the last song, they were already starting late.

Ten minutes turned to fifteen. Then fifteen turned to twenty. By the time she took her position on stage, there was no way she'd finish in time to see me off.

I stood at the edge of the stage, just out of view of the audience, in the spot that had become mine when I got to watch Maya perform. I was out of sight, but as close as I could be to her without getting in the way.

Maya was a goddess in her bodysuit that shimmered under the bright stage lights. The music pulsed through the air, pulling all eyes to her while she sang, danced, and brought the whole stadium alive.

"She's good," a guy said from beside me.

I turned, and Bax, the lead singer for Dimefront, watched beside me in a worn leather jacket, the sleeves pushed up to reveal tattoos snaking around his arms.

"She's more than good," I replied, staring back at her. From the way she moved with such grace and power. From the way her voice filled the entire stadium.

"She cares about you a lot," Bax said, his eyes never leaving the stage.

"I love her," I said.

Bax scratched at the bridge of his nose. "Love can lift a person

161

up to the top or pull them to the bottom. It's fickle like that." Bax shrugged, clapping me on the back. "Falling in love changes shit, ya know?"

I did. I knew.

Elliott showed up as a living reminder of the ticking clock, telling me my time was up, and I wouldn't get that goodbye. Between songs, Maya looked at me, caught my eye, and winked.

She still had hope.

"We gotta go," Elliott said.

I'd already bought an extra five minutes by promising him double on his annual bonus, but that time was done.

Maya caught my gaze again. I pointed to my watch, then gave a half-hearted wave.

Her expression fell only the slightest before she composed herself. She didn't miss a step as I walked away.

This was how it would be for us, with the lives we chose. We would just have to make it work because I wouldn't pull her down.

CHAPTER
TWENTY-FIVE

MAYA

It took a decent amount of finagling, but Elliott and Hans had worked out the schedule for Sloan and me. We were officially on a thirty-day fast until our calendars aligned again.

I hated it. Sloan hated it.

But we couldn't exactly reschedule a pro football game or leave Dimefront without an opening act for their concerts.

So, we played phone tag and texted all the time. After a particularly hard day, my phone finally rang. His name popped up on the screen, and I answered immediately.

"Sloan." I stood from the couch on my tour bus to escape to the back, where it was private. The soft hum of the engine beneath me provided a steady backdrop to the distant sounds of the traffic outside.

My sleeping space in the back was dimly lit, with a petite leather couch along one side and a small bed along the other. Not Four Seasons fancy but definitely functional.

"Baby, I miss you." His words were gruff, and he sounded exhausted.

CHRISTINA HOVLAND

The bus gently swayed as it navigated a sharp turn, and the streetlights from outside slashed fleeting stripes across the space.

"Sorry about the game." It hadn't gone well. They lost by a lot, and he took several hits.

"It happens. You can't win 'em all." He groaned, and it wasn't a good groan.

"We don't have to talk about that," I assured.

"Talk about anything. I just need to hear your voice," he said.

"Are you hurt?" I asked, sitting cross-legged on the bed. "You sound like you're in pain."

"Took a hard hit to the ribs. Just sore," he admitted. "It's part of the game."

A pang of concern fluttered in my chest, along with an image of the worst hit he took today. "You need to get that checked out."

"Promise, it's not a big deal," he said, his voice husky. "I wish I could be there with you."

"Me, too," I agreed, absentmindedly plucking at a piece of lint on the knee of my jeans. "When things like this happen—the game goes bad and you come out bruised—do you ever think that maybe the field is better during practice when it's all pretend, and it doesn't really count?"

"Who says practice doesn't count?" he asked.

"You know what I mean. Do you think maybe Vegas during the day is safer because it's easy? And Vegas at night might be prettier, but it's not worth the risk of getting mugged?" I asked.

He seemed to chew on that question. "I'm wondering if maybe they both have their place."

"You can't have the wins without the losses kind of thing?" I asked.

"No, it's not that. Because you can absolutely have the wins without the losses. I'm just thinking that only because it's day doesn't mean it's any worse than night. It's just perception. I can get bruised during the day, too."

"But at night, when you get hurt, everyone is watching," I said.

164

"That's the truth," he said, as his covers rustled in the background.

I missed him. Damn, but I missed him. I missed the half-smirk of his smile and the way he tried to get me to go outside when I didn't want to.

"I didn't go outside today," I said. "I mean, I did for the show and walking to the stadium, but..."

"You didn't see any deer," he finished for me.

"No, there are no deer in downtown Chicago, apparently," I said, kind of sad about that. "Didn't see a chipmunk or a bobcat or anything. Not even a super-neat boulder."

"When we get back home, I'm so going to take you to my special rock." He laughed low.

"That sounds like you're trying to turn me on," I said.

"Do I have to try?" He laughed. "Then I'm losing my touch."

He wasn't. Not at all.

We sat in silence for a long while, letting our quiet keep the other company.

"Hey, guess what I totally spaced?" I asked.

I didn't wait for him to respond.

"Jared's wedding is next week, and I've been so self-involved that I forgot. I can't believe I forgot."

"Jared?"

"My old friend? Served us chicken fluff at his engagement party before we drank questionable margaritas? I was going to stalk his cousin at the wedding but now I don't have to?"

"Right. Jared."

"I totally forgot about his wedding," I said, again.

"You forgot, or you moved forward with your life?" Sloan asked, gently but with purpose.

"I think I moved forward," I said. Wasn't that the surprise of surprises... "I mean, I'll send them a nice gift from us."

"Nice, but not too nice," Sloan said with a chuckle. "A decent amount of nice."

The conversation lingered between us, a silent understanding passing through the phone lines as we held onto each other's words.

"I'm gonna go catch some sleep," Sloan finally said.

"Sure, yes, rest," I agreed, nodding even though he couldn't see me.

And that was it. There was no demand from our bodies to do more or to find a release with each other. Just talking to each other was enough after a bad day.

And dammit, I was worried about him.

I was worried about him because…

Nope.

I wouldn't allow myself to go there.

I couldn't be in love with my husband.

Except I was pretty sure I was, and I needed to figure out how to deal with that. Sometime, in the recent past, I'd gone and let my heart get involved. This was about realizing that I had feelings for him, and I seriously didn't know what to do with that.

And then I realized what had to happen, and it couldn't wait thirty days. I needed to talk to Hans.

Lucky for me, Hans didn't keep normal working hours, so when the buses pulled up to the next stop, and I knocked on his door, he let me in.

Hans was built like a lineman, but he dressed like an investor always heading into an important meeting. So it was odd to see him without his tie and suit jacket. Though he probably didn't wear those all the time—especially when he was basically off duty.

"What's going on, Maya?" he asked, gesturing for me to join him.

"I need to go see Sloan," I said. I hadn't run to Hans' bus or anything, but I was still out of breath as I spoke. "It's important, and it's a conversation that needs to happen in person."

Hans frowned.

"Hans, it's important," I said, emphasizing the last word.

"Let me see what I can come up with," he agreed. "How soon do you need to be there?"

That was sort of the problem, wasn't it?

"As soon as possible?"

Hans frowned deeper and thought about it. "I could maybe make Thursday happen? Get you there, get you back before the show?"

I grimaced. "He's got a game."

"Then we'll have to finagle the times. You sure this is something that can't wait?" he confirmed.

"Yes," I said. "No. I mean, it can't wait. Sooner is better."

CHAPTER
TWENTY-SIX

MAYA

The week dragged on, but Thursday finally came. The black Cadillac SUV with tinted windows rolled up near where the tour buses sat parked outside the stadium. I started to sweat, but not from the heat. I brushed back my hair to keep it from sticking to my forehead. I felt a little sick, and it wasn't about divorce or annulments.

"Thank you," I said to Hans. He would've come along with me to Denver, but he had to stay and keep things moving here.

"You have one hour there, and then you're back on a plane. Straight here for the next show." Hans opened the door, holding his hand out to help me into the vehicle.

It took some work to figure out the logistics on this trip, and he wasn't thrilled about it, but he understood that I needed this salt and pepper conversation with my husband.

He made it happen.

That's how I found myself settled into the backseat of the SUV, pulling up to Dimefront's private jet at the airport. Everything about the way the world looked seemed to be subtly muted right then. Like somebody had pushed the sofa too far to the left, and the flow was all jacked up.

I left the car and scooted across the tarmac while calling Finn.

"Finn?" I asked into my cell. "I need a favor."

"Shoot, whatcha got?" Finn asked without seeing what the favor might be.

"I need you to give Sloan a jar of pepper tonight." I started up the stairs to the plane, though it wouldn't be leaving until it was time. I still took them quickly. "After the game."

"Pepper?" he asked, surprised.

"Sloan will know what it means, and it's important. Can you do it for me?"

Finn hesitated, and a low-grade panic crept up on me. I needed to hear his yes, not hesitation.

"Please. It's how he'll know it's important that I'm there," I said.

"You're coming to see the game?" Finn asked, perking up.

Gah. "No, I'll be cutting it short and getting there right after."

"Bummer," Finn said. "Would love to see you on the Jumbotron sometime."

I shivered in agreement.

"Me, too," I echoed.

"And this pepper thing is a kinky bit you two have going on?" Finn asked, like he was being nonchalant but nosey. "Like he sprinkles you, or you sprinkle him?"

Finn's questions weren't helping my pre-flight, pre-important-talk stress levels.

"You're not helping this situation," I said, taking a seat in the middle of the plane and buckling up.

"There's a situation? All I know is I answered my phone."

"Finn." I didn't mean to be short, but I was. "Please. I need your help."

"Then consider it done. Jar of pepper after the game. Can I tell him it's from you?" he asked.

"Yes. Please." Nobody else should be giving him seasoning in

169

the locker room, but might as well make it clear where it came from.

"Does it have to be full? Or can I just bring the one from home?" Finn asked, and it sounded like he was rummaging through a cupboard.

"It doesn't have to be full," I assured as the plane taxied for takeoff.

The flight was uneventful, though I spent most of it staring out the window, thinking about what came next.

We landed, and I stepped off the private jet, the brisk Colorado air welcoming me home. Hans was right, though—I had little time.

I hurried to the waiting black van that would take me to Stallion Stadium.

While I didn't make it for the game, they won, and Sloan didn't take any particularly hard hits today. I got ushered through a maze of hallways until we reached a small locker room office. It's the only place I could meet Sloan on such short notice and on such a tight timeline. Small with dim lighting, the air in here was thick with the smell of sweat and leather.

That's where I waited, staring into space and hoping my husband was on his way as the clock ticked on the wall.

"Maya?" Sloan said my name as he approached the door to his coach's office, a mix of surprise and worry mingling in his expression. "You're here."

"I'm here." I took him in, checking him from top to bottom. I was worried about his injury from the last game. He looked good, though—healthy, even, and fresh from a post-game shower.

But I didn't rush to him, like usual. When we touched each other, our bodies took over, and for this kind of conversation, we needed clear heads.

"You, uh, left me a message?" He held up a half-empty jar of pepper.

"Things feel off between us. I think we need to talk. Really talk and open the conversation back up." My voice wobbled as I spoke.

He set the pepper down on the corner of the desk, poking it away from the edge with the tip of his finger.

"Let's talk." He tried to sound casual, but the concern for where I was going with this was obvious in the way he couldn't quite meet my gaze.

"You said you loved me." Why was my heart racing? This was only a conversation.

"I said that I'm in love with you," he corrected me calmly.

"Is there a difference?" I asked.

"I think so. I love lots of things, but I'm not in love with them. Seriously love this team, love winning games, love when I'm having Lucky Charms and it's all marshmallows at the end. But I'm not in love with any of those things," he explained with a small smile.

"Sloan, I don't know what you want me to say to this. I've done the love thing. I've spent most of my life being in love with love. But it never worked. What we have here, it works without the love part," I said, earnestly. "It works."

"And I've fallen in love with you, so it's changed. Doesn't mean it won't keep working," he clarified.

He seemed so certain. Why couldn't I be certain, too?

"Maya," he said my name, and I knew whatever came next, it wouldn't make me comfortable.

"Are you in love with me?" he asked directly, searching my face for an answer.

"It doesn't even matter if I am, because that's not what we agreed on." I crossed my arms, then uncrossed them.

"Are you in this?" he pressed on. "Or are we just going through the motions?"

"I've been in this," I replied, hurt and ticked off that he'd imply I hadn't been.

"Things have changed. I want more," he said matter-of-factly.

"Sloan, this isn't what we agreed to," I reminded him, a sense of panic rising in my chest.

"That's why we're talking about it now, isn't it?" he reasoned.

171

"Is this because we're apart so much? Because there will be an off season, and the tour will end," I assured. "It'll be just like before."

"You're right. I realized I fell in love with you because of the distance between us and the way it feels missing you. But it only amplified everything I already felt. It didn't create the feelings." He stopped to think about that. "I don't want to live apart like this all the time. But I'm also not stupid enough to ignore the fact that we both have jobs that take us away from each other. That's just how it is. The reason you have to leave? It's part of why I love you. And the reason I have to leave? Pretty sure you get that it's not only a game to me. Football is part of who I am," he explained, his voice tinged with feeling as he spoke.

"What are you asking me for?" I finally asked. "What do you want from me?"

"I... I just want to know if you're in this." He seemed so vulnerable with the way he fidgeted with the pepper shaker on the desk. "You aren't in love with me? I can live with that. But know that it doesn't change things for how I feel about you."

"Yes, yes, Sloan. I'm in this." I said the words, but even I didn't quite believe them.

"If something matters to you, it matters to me," Sloan reassured. "Don't doubt that. Don't doubt the way you feel, either."

"This was always supposed to be a marriage of convenience," I said. "But it's not feeling very convenient anymore, is it?"

He scanned the room, his eyes meeting mine and then falling to the pepper shaker. "I wanted no expectations. I meant it, and I expect nothing from you, either, other than we're honest with each other."

"I came because we need to decide if this—if us—still works," I said.

"Is this a breakup?" he asked, point blank.

I moved to him, then, until we were right there in each other's personal space.

"This is not a breakup," I assured. "I'm not leaving you. I'm not ending anything. This is like a… heads up for us both."

"I am all in," he said. "But are you? Are you, really?"

I didn't know how to answer that. I wanted to say that I loved him, too, but there was so much more to what we had than that.

"Sloan," I said his name since I didn't know what else to say.

He reached for me, and I let him pull me to his chest. My throat worked as he pressed a kiss to the top of my head.

The question lingered… Was I all in?

He tilted my chin and breathed a light kiss against my lips, testing things out. I opened for him and kissed him right back. Pressed against him in that little room, I questioned everything about what I'd found to be true.

I'd thought that maybe if I rearranged my life like furniture, it'd get better. And it did.

But now, Sloan wanted to move the furniture again, and I had to figure out if I was okay with it and if I'd help him. Or if I was stuck again.

CHAPTER
TWENTY-SEVEN

SLOAN

Maya left for the airport, and I hung out in the locker room. I didn't want to go to my Denver apartment, and there was no way I could go home to the house I thought of as ours. Not without her tonight.

I sat on an empty bench in the empty locker room, feeling pretty damn empty.

"What's up, dog?" Finn tapped the side of a locker with his fist as he came into the room. "Maya still here?"

I shook my head. "She had to get back."

"I'm guessing the pepper shit wasn't something you're into?" Finn nodded knowingly. "I was worried about that."

"Jackass," I said with a chuckle. "It's the code we use when we need to have a serious conversation about the rules of us."

"Well, fuck," Finn said, dropping to sit on the bench across from me. "That makes me feel like a grade-A jackass. And it sounds way less fun than what I was thinking."

"I think she's pulling away from me," I said. "I told her I'm in love with her, and she's pulling away."

Finn let out a long whistle. "I'm firmly against telling anyone

174

you're in love with them. Best to keep that shit locked tight, if you ask me."

"Kid, that's why you're single." Coach strode into the locker room, his hands on his hips. He looked right at me but jerked his thumb toward Finn. "Don't listen to people who don't know what it's like to make a woman happy."

"I know what it's like," Finn said in defense.

"What's it like then, Romeo?" Coach asked.

Then he waited for Finn to come up with an answer we all knew would be bullshit.

"I think I'll just sit here and let you two talk," Finn said, stretching out on the bench to stare at the fluorescent lights above us, his hands linked behind his head.

"Good call," Coach said. Then he pointed at me. "What'd you do?"

"What makes you think I did anything?" I asked, eyebrows drawing together. Now, it was my turn to be on the defensive.

"Given you're the one pouting in the locker room while everyone else is out celebrating the win, I'd say you did something. Tell me I'm wrong." Coach didn't sit. Then again, he never sat. He leaned against the lockers, which was about as relaxed as I'd ever seen him, really. Like he was all settled in and ready for a good story.

"I told my wife that I'm in love with her," I said, and if that was wrong, then I didn't know how to be right.

Coach pursed his lips, nodded. "What'd she say to that?"

"She flew out here to ask me if I meant it and to find out how that changed things." I cleared my throat. "We'd agreed when we got married in Vegas to leave love out of it. Agreed that things would be easier if we kept love out of it."

I told him all of it, about how we'd accidentally gotten married. The rules of the marriage and how it'd gone so well until now.

"Well, that's stupid," Coach said, dismissive as fuck. "You're a goddamned idiot, but you did something right because she came halfway across the country to figure it out with you."

"I fucked up because it was easy, until I opened my mouth and asked for a new game plan," I said.

"Marriage is easy?" Coach asked. "That's what you thought?"

The question sounded rhetorical, but he said nothing more, and Finn said nothing, so I said—

"Yes?" It was a kind of statement and a question.

"Kid, marriage is like a football career." Coach narrowed his eyes at me and pointed his finger. "You think a football career that starts easy stays easy?" He didn't wait for an answer. "Fuck no, it doesn't. Work. A person can have all the talent in the world and with that natural ability, they cruise through high school and become a champion. Get a scholarship to college. But then the actual work will have to start, and you know it."

Damn, he was getting worked up and red in the face.

"Did you cruise your way into professional football? Into getting drafted, traded four fucking times, before I brought you here? Or did you have to work for it?" At that point, he was yelling.

He waited, so I guessed it was my turn to talk again. "I worked for it."

Worked my ass off through the grief of losing my family, through broken ribs and sprained ankles.

"Exactly, you worked for it. Nobody handed you this career. Nobody hands you a good marriage. Work for it."

I'd heard Coach compare football to almost everything, but I'd never heard his take on football and marriage before.

"You should listen to him," Finn said. "His wife seems pretty happy."

"Because when she has a rough patch and questions shit—and don't think that's never happened—I try harder. I'm her husband. That's my goddamned job."

"I need to try harder?" I asked, to clarify that I understood exactly what he was going for with this lecture.

"Yes, kid, you need to try harder. You say you love her, but how did you show her? Seems to me she flew all the way here tonight to talk to you—my guess is she's in love with you, too, because if you didn't matter to her, she would've picked up the goddamned phone and kept it simple. Sent you a text. A woman doesn't fly across the country for a thirty-minute conversation unless she's pissed as hell, or she's in love with you." He turned to Finn. "Was she pissed as hell?"

He shook his head. "Not that I saw."

"Well, you'd know. That one's easy to spot," Coach retorted.

"How do you show someone you love them when you're thousands of miles away?" I asked, genuinely curious.

"How the fuck do I know?" Coach asked. "But you're in the big leagues now, kid. That means you've got to come up with an MVP husband performance. Something she'll understand, and something that's from your goddamned heart. A sweeping victory declaration of how you're ready to fight for the two of you."

"I could call a press conference," I said.

Coach shook his head. "Too impersonal."

"I could take out a billboard in the next town she's in." I was grasping at straws but trying to figure this out. "And the next after that."

Coach tilted his head from shoulder to shoulder. "That's better, but does it have any special significance for you and her?"

I shook my head. "No."

Finn was sitting now with a shit-eating grin on his face. He raised his hand like we were in a fifth-grade classroom and not in a professional football locker room.

"Better be good," Coach grumbled.

"You should make a viral dance on social media," Finn said, dropping his hand. "Call it the Slaya."

"It's good that you know how to catch a ball," Coach said, shaking his head.

"Actually..." Now, I was sitting taller. "The whole reason we ended up staying married is because it got posted on social media. Finn might be onto something."

"See?" Finn said. "I'm more than a pretty face who catches footballs."

"What if I sang one of her songs back to her?" I asked.

"What if you wrote her a song?" Finn countered.

"I don't write songs," I said. "But... I guess I could try?"

Or... actually, I knew just what to do. I wouldn't win a Grammy or anything, but maybe it'd be enough to make my point.

"We need to get T.J. and Darius looped in," I said. "They're into creative shit."

"They love this stuff," Finn agreed.

"You two have it under control." Coach started toward the exit with a backward wave. "Don't fuck it up." Then he turned on his heel. "Your contract got renewed. Came to tell you. Elliott has details. Don't fuck that up, either. Don't fuck anything up."

CHAPTER
TWENTY-EIGHT

MAYA

The Stallions' path to the playoffs was uncertain. They weren't in, not yet. Tomorrow, they had to win this one crucial game to secure their spot, and it was against the team they'd lost so horribly to in the game where Sloan got hurt.

Sloan's attention was entirely consumed by training and team strategies, making our interactions sporadic at best. I understood he was doing what needed done, and I knew they'd come out of this with a win. Of course, the Stallions weren't celebrating prematurely. They also weren't wallowing in self-doubt. Instead, all of their energy, all of their determination, all the team focus got channeled toward winning tomorrow's wild card game.

I'd hoped having the conversation with Sloan would bring some clarity to what we were doing in our marriage. But it only seemed to stir up the mud and make everything murky. Murky and infused with a kind of awkward I didn't like at all.

I couldn't see where I was going with him, and I was worried.

The good news for me was that this leg of the Dimefront tour ended in Vegas. So, after the last show, I headed to Mom and

Dad's with them. They came to the concert, and it was outstanding to have them backstage with me, seeing what I'd become.

Then I was back home with them in the house where I grew up. Vegas might not be home anymore, but it was still nice to be back in the city I grew up in and not be a backup for anyone. There was nostalgia here that brought back memories I'd nearly forgotten.

And yet, my first task was reaching out to Sloan.

> Maya: Tour 1st leg done ✓✓

> Sloan: ...

> Maya: How was today?

> Sloan: ...

> Maya: Call when you're done w/ mtngs

"Come to our house in Estes Park," I said, helping Mom chop lettuce for the dinner salad. The normalcy of the task made me warm inside, since my life recently was filled with more of the extraordinary than the normal. Things like helping in the kitchen felt comforting for a change.

Seeing Mom and reveling in the end of the tour leg might not have been the same dopamine rush as performing in a stadium, but it filled a void I hadn't quite realized needed filling. After the past months of going full speed, this time was like a bowl of chicken noodle soup after months of fancy meals. There was something comforting about being in a space where the countertops stayed cluttered with jars of herbs and spices, and stacks of mail lay in piles along the edge. There was comfort in the imperfections.

"I don't know," Mom said, moving through her kitchen with

ease. "I'm more of a city girl. The whole idea of nature doesn't really excite me."

"Sloan will convince you," I said, grabbing a tomato for the salad. "The man is very convincing. He even got me outside." I paused the chopping. "Turns out that I actually really like the mountains. I can't even describe how the air just feels better there."

Mom stared at me for a long beat. "I always wondered when I'd see you happy like this."

"Like what?" I mean, I was happy, but it wasn't like I was unhappy before.

"Like this. You light up when you talk about Sloan, and you talk about him like he's the best thing in the world."

"He is," I said, realizing that I believed it wholeheartedly. "He's the best thing that ever happened to me, at least."

"Then we should go to the mountains. See your house and meet your husband," Dad said, grabbing a hunk of carrot from the corner of my cutting board.

My parents had been together since they were in college. They'd been through most of their lives as a team.

"Why do you think you two work so well?" I asked. They were definitely in love—they looked at each other like the other could do no wrong. And they vocalized their love all the time.

"Everybody wants the love story, but nobody wants the dirty socks that come three years later." Mom poked at the chicken in the pan on the stove. "Or sometimes, three months later. But, sweetheart, when you have a true love story, you don't care about the dirty socks today, tomorrow, or three years from now. It's never about the socks."

"Sloan and I have talked about how there's the good part and then the not-so-great part of things and experiences. Like The Strip at night is so pretty with all the lights, but during the day, it looks like someone is trying way too hard to convince us it's just as good," I mused.

"It's the same place, just different. Doesn't make it better or worse. Yeah, the lights are pretty until you're tired and want to get some sleep. Then they won't stop flashing." Mom reached into the cupboard to grab a stack of plates. "Then Vegas during the day, when it's quieter, sure sounds like a better deal."

"You think?" I hadn't thought of it like that.

"Sloan and I talked about how the stage before the show was so boring and only a collection of wood and metal, but it's peaceful. Calm, even," I said. "And the field before the game has a feeling of gentle excitement that swells to full volume during the event." That gentle excitement made a person's stomach flutter with anticipation. "I'm in love with Sloan," I admitted. "I really am."

Mom raised her eyebrows. "You weren't aware of this? I think the entire country has been aware of this for some time now."

"Yes, I, uh… I guess I hadn't been ready to admit it. I suppose I need to tell him that."

"Third time's a charm?" Dad asked.

I nodded, because I wanted the professional football player, the guy who encouraged me to go outside and try something new. The guy who shared parts of himself with me that weren't for everyone else. I didn't want only the parts of him that were safe. I wanted the whole man.

"I'm so proud of you." Mom's eyes misted. "You've really blossomed into yourself."

Mom was right. I wasn't stuck in the back, watching everyone else move ahead anymore. I was leading the way, and I had a pretty exceptional man right there with me.

"You deserve this kind of love," Dad added, putting his arm around Mom's shoulders.

We settled in to eat dinner, and the murky water I'd been treading seemed to clear. I knew what I wanted. Understood that with Sloan, we could change the rules, and it wouldn't change anything. Because at the end of the tour or the season—we were in love with each other.

If he'd just freaking call me. Or text me. Or something.

Unfortunately, Mom's rule of no phones at the dinner table even applied to pop princesses waiting for their husbands to call.

When my cell chimed from the counter, I practically dropped my fork, standing so quickly.

"It's probably Sloan," I said as a way of explanation for my quick maneuvering to the counter.

It wasn't Sloan.

Emily had sent me a link, and while links could wait, out of habit, I clicked on it.

The world turned topsy-turvy because there was Sloan filling the screen with the perpetual smirk I loved so much.

Sloan staring at me from the Stallions social media account, sitting next to T.J. in the middle of the locker room, with Darius on his other side, and the rest of the guys behind them. T.J. held a guitar and strummed the opening chords to Ingrid Michaelson's *The Way You Are*.

The same song I sang to the engaged couple the night Sloan and I got married. Damn, I choked up and didn't even try to stop the tears from falling.

Sloan couldn't find the pitch, but he sure as hell tried.

As he sang off-key, T.J. kept him going with the melody on the guitar, and the guys all behind him tapped out the percussion like they were backup musicians and not professional football players.

Then Darius slid the blank poster board away and there in bold letters, it read:

#Slaya

As Sloan continued to sing, Darius tapped his foot to the beat and nodded his head to the melody, continuing to slip away the top poster board to reveal what it said underneath.

A pre-game love song for my wife.
Because
She
Means
Everything
To

Me

The last note hung in the air, and the screen faded to black.

I set the phone down on the counter, feeling everything I'd been too scared to feel for Sloan.

"You know." Dad cleared his throat and smiled a wry grin. "I enjoy football, and I've been watching the Stallions this year. Wouldn't mind taking in a game sometime. I hear there's a good one tomorrow."

"Is that a hint?" I asked, wiping away a tear or four.

"Well, if you're gonna go to the game and cheer him on from the stands?" Dad asked. "Maybe you need someone to keep you company?"

As amazing as that sounded, my heart dipped because—

"I can't." I shook my head. "They need me at the studio in Los Angeles to start prep for recording the album."

"You can't record in Denver?" Dad asked with a frown. "Where your husband is?"

Was that a choice? No one had offered it as an option.

"I don't know, actually," I said, gnawing at my lip.

Honestly, I didn't know. Hans told me where to be, and I made that happen. I didn't even consider that I could have a choice in the matter. But, actually, I probably had a say.

The Dimefront guys all recorded in Denver, so I knew there was a studio there with the capability. I just hadn't thought about asking.

I would remedy that immediately.

"I think I should go to Sloan's game instead of Los Angeles, don't you?" I asked, smiling at my dad. "And, yes, I'll definitely need company."

CHAPTER
TWENTY-NINE

SLOAN

Maya didn't pick up my call last night, and she didn't respond to the video, either. All I got was a note that things got crazy, and we'd talk after today's game. She added a smiley face for good measure.

She had to have seen the video because everybody and their dog had seen the video. It went mega viral, super quick, and fans went crazy for #Slaya.

But that was yesterday, and today, the guys and I jogged onto the field like we always did at the beginning of the game. The hit of excitement from the crowd as they all stomped their feet was a drug that couldn't be replicated.

Our quarterback, Drake Wellington, handled the coin toss for us when the song we sang to Maya blared over the speakers of the stadium. They hadn't used my version, which was good because Coach told me it was a good thing I could catch a ball since I had no future in music.

The stadium went even more wired, even more wild, and I scanned to see what they were so worked up about.

It didn't take me but a second to see that Maya was on the

Jumbotron, wearing my jersey with the number forty-one, a blue ZipZing in one hand, and a sign in the other that read:

In it to win it. Let's go #Slaya

My breath stuck in my ribs.

She was in it with me.

Damn, I blew out the breath because I needed to keep my head where it belonged. But she was cheering like it was her full-time job, and I couldn't tear my gaze away from the image of her.

She's here.

She came to watch me win. So, dammit, I had a game to win.

"Are we writing love songs, or are we going to the goddamned playoffs?" Coach yelled from right beside me, right into my ear.

"Going to the goddamned playoffs," I shouted back, letting the adrenaline of the moment take hold so I could do my job, see the team make the playoffs, and go home with my wife.

So, that was what I did. Or rather, I'd started by helping my team win the game. Then I got stuck in an interview room with a bunch of reporters asking a fuck-ton of questions.

"Question from *The Denver Herald*," a reporter said, holding up his pen.

I nodded. "Hit me."

"We've all seen your team reel online," the guy said.

I nodded.

The guy didn't keep talking, so I asked, "Did you have a question?"

"What was Ms. Mitchell's response to the song?" he asked.

"Did you have a question about the game?" I asked, dodging the question because, well, I didn't want to answer it. Not yet anyway. Not until I got the hell out of there and got to see her.

"Given the time you've spent apart, are you concerned about your relationship with Ms. Mitchell?" the reporter asked, keeping on the same track.

And wasn't that just pounding the nail on the head and hitting my thumb with the hammer, all at the same time?

"I'm not here to talk about my personal life. I'm here to talk about the game." I paused, and then I continued, saying straight into the microphone, "A game we won."

"I'm wondering, too," a voice said from the back.

That voice I'd know anywhere. Maya was... right damn there in front of me, about halfway up the aisle. Right in the fucking middle of the swarm of reporters.

"The message on social media wasn't for the world. It was for you," I said. "How, uh, did you like it?"

Damn, but my voice got gravelly, and my heart beat so hard, the mic probably picked it up and broadcast it across all the networks and into the world at large.

"You should keep playing football," she said, with a twinkle in her eye.

Everyone in the room seemed to laugh, including me.

"And about the other?" a reporter shouted.

"I'm always concerned about the time I'm not with you, Maya," I said, finally answering the reporter, but staring straight at my girl while I spoke. "Always."

"But when you love someone, you figure out a way to make it work, right?" Maya asked.

This was happening. Fucking happening right here, right now, in the middle of the press conference, and none of the public relations handlers were doing a damn thing to step in and give me a moment to catch my breath.

And that was the moment I realized I didn't need to catch my breath anymore. Because I wasn't holding it anymore.

That was the moment I started to breathe.

"When you love someone," I said, holding her gaze to mine since I couldn't jump over the table and hold her to me. "Figuring it out is the fun part."

The edges of her lips tilted up at the sides, and her eyes misted. And, you know what? Fuck it.

CHRISTINA HOVLAND

There wasn't one rule that said I couldn't jump over the damn table if it meant I'd get to my wife.

So, I did.

Vaulted right over the sonofabitch and moved straight to my Maya.

Maya, whose eyes had gotten huge about the time I'd slid my ass across the table and knocked off a few microphones in the process.

"What are you doing?" she asked, breathy as all hell and gorgeous as all fuck.

"I came to kiss my wife."

The room stilled, some kind of universal pause button having been pushed about the time I decided to follow through on every single promise I'd ever made, and every single promise I'd ever make to this woman.

She sucked in a quick breath of air, which was good because she'd need it while I kissed the hell out of her. Right there in front of the media. In front of my teammates. In front of the entire fucking world.

Because, dammit, this was the fun part.

"You know," I said, in her ear so only she could hear, "I heard once that women like to have their respect served with a side of tongue. That still hold true?"

Maya nodded, unable to find words. Which wasn't a problem, because with what I had planned, we wouldn't need them.

"Sloan," Elliott practically shouted my name, cutting through this fucking fabulous moment between Maya and me.

I turned, only because he'd always had my back and while his timing was shit, he'd never truly let me down.

"Hot mic," he said, pointing to his lapel.

I glanced at the microphone clipped to my shirt and said, "Fuck."

"I think they heard about the respect served with a side of tongue," Maya whispered. Which she didn't need to do because

188

my lapel microphone would pick it up no matter what her volume.

"I love you," she said, not whispering. "I love singing in stadiums, and I love my ZipZings, but I'm in love with you, Sloan Stevens, and there's no way I'm doing life without you."

"You think you're still in love with the idea of being in love?" I asked, not even serious because I knew the answer already.

"I'm not in love with the idea of marriage or even getting married." She smiled as she pressed her forehead to mine. "Or being in love with being in love." She held my gaze with hers as she said, "I'm in love with you, Sloan Stevens. For better or for worse."

"Mine," I said, leaning in to pull her for a kiss.

She broke it only long enough to say, "All yours. And you're mine, too."

Yes, yes, I was.

Instead of saying something smart or just saying nothing at all, I ripped the damn microphone off, pulled the wires free, and then I picked Maya up in my arms.

"Did you actually add product placement to your declaration of love for me?" I asked, chuckling.

"I figured it couldn't hurt when you finally have that meeting with them." She smiled against my mouth.

I carried her like we'd just gotten married, and there was a threshold or some shit like that—her arms around my neck and my grip holding her tight.

That was how we left the press conference.

Sure, there were lots of reporters shouting questions at us. But we didn't stop to answer any of them, not when we had a moment together where I could respect the hell out of my wife.

My wife.

That would never get old.

EPILOGUE

MAYA

I woke up staring at Elvis.

Or rather, the bust of Elvis in the corner of the condo where Sloan and I had first met. We were back in Vegas since it had been three hundred and sixty-five days since we first woke up hitched in this city.

Today, we were both naked again. But this time, we'd made it back to the condo, and there was no panic. No worry about an annulment or a divorce or how everyone would react to the news.

"'Morning, gorgeous," Sloan said softly in my ear, his arms wrapped around me. "Happy anniversary."

I turned in his arms, so we were nose to nose, skin to skin, chest to chest. "Happy anniversary, handsome."

"You feelin' like getting married again?" he asked as he brushed butterfly kisses against my cheek on his trek downward, past the column of my throat, along my collarbone.

"Well"—I snuggled in closer to the warmth that was my husband to give him better access—"Not to brag or anything, but it is kind of my thing when I come to town."

He chuckled, low and deep in his chest. "As long as I get to be the groom."

"Always," I said, and the truth of the word came out with a lifetime's worth of emotion.

I couldn't say much after that because his mouth was on my breast, and his hand was between my legs, and there were other things that took precedence over coherent speech.

The thing was, we'd made an entire year of memories we never wanted to forget, but there was one part both of us couldn't quite shake.

Neither of us remembered how it started. We decided that wouldn't work for us, so we set up a vow renewal for our anniversary. Together, and sober, we'd recreate some memories we could actually remember this time.

We were going to re-do that whole night, knowing what we'd pieced together and bringing along as many friends as possible. Even Jared and his wife were meeting up with us. Mom and Dad, my sisters, Emily, Elliott, Uncle Milo, Aunt Lisa, Angela, Finn, and most of the Stallions football team had even come to town for the big event. Heck, the Dimefront guys, Sami Jo, *and* Hans were all on hand.

No one wanted to miss this backward charade of ours.

But that morning, it was only Sloan and me, the two of us cocooned in our own world.

We took full advantage of our time together—twice, actually.

After we came up for air, we headed out to spend the day with our friends. And when the afternoon became evening, our entourage of football players, family, and one of the biggest bands of our generation headed out on the town. We caused more than a minor commotion as we walked down The Strip to the Neon Nuptials wedding chapel. Let's just say the guy who played Tarzan had nothing on the chaos we caused simply by being present.

With a small amount of research, we discovered we'd been

married at the Neon Nuptials with their Lucky in Love and Liberace package. So, that was what we booked this time.

The chapel itself was unassuming. Given the name, I figured that there would be more neon involved. But the chapel seemed to rely on the surrounding neon to live up to its name.

The interior was well-maintained, with a bright-red carpet that seemed to bleed a crimson path to happiness and white wooden pews with an undeniable charm, probably because of all they'd witnessed over the years. Over the top of the room was a painted ceiling that looked like stars.

Our crew squeezed into the limited space, everyone huddling together. The paparazzi might be outside, clamoring for a glimpse of our private celebration, but within the walls, only those closest to us mattered.

Those closest to us—and an actor playing Liberace.

The fake Liberace guy was the spitting image of the musician, with his sequined suit sparkling under the lights in the chapel. His perfectly styled hair and signature candelabra ring were like a time warp to another era.

"This is the singing couple!" Fake Liberace announced as we approached the altar at the front of the room. "I remember you like yesterday."

"Maya has the pipes, that's for sure." Sloan pulled me against his side and pressed a kiss to my hair.

"What did I sing?" I asked, hoping he might remember the song so I could give an impromptu performance to my husband.

But Fake Liberace's eyebrows creased together. "No, it was you"—he pointed to Sloan— "who wouldn't stop singing for the whole ceremony. Oh, we laughed and laughed."

Now, Sloan's eyebrows dropped. "There's no way—"

"What did he sing?" I asked, before Sloan could finish his sentence. "I have to know what his song was."

Liberace gestured widely as he said, "He kept singing about me feeling it, and you feeling it, and putting on lipstick."

I turned to the rockers in the audience. "Anyone know?"

Everyone shook their heads in unison.

"Do you remember the tune?" I asked, losing some hope since it wasn't something easy to recall, like *Viva Las Vegas* or *Love Me Tender*.

Fake Liberace started humming. and—

"Lady Gaga's *Manicure* song," Bax said with a chin jerk to Sloan. "Nice choice."

"I don't know that song," Sloan said. "I swear I don't know that song."

Bax sang the melody, the other Dimefront guys getting in on it for a few bars.

"Drunk Sloan clearly knows more music than sober Sloan," I said, blinking innocently.

Sloan stared at the audience, then at me when they paused singing.

"I've never heard that before in my life," he assured.

"That isn't true," Liberace said, pointing his finger toward Bax. "We both know the truth." Fake Liberace winked at Sloan, his mischievous eyes twinkling. "Shall we proceed with the ceremony?"

Sloan nodded, a grin playing on his lips. "Please and thank you."

I smiled up at him, a surge of love and excitement settling in my heart as I got to experience a wedding ceremony I'd actually get to remember this time.

We did the "Do yous?" and the "I dos" and there was an impromptu performance by our officiant before he got to the "Kiss her" part.

The whole time, Sloan and I grinned like we'd both had two of those yardstick margaritas.

"And now, by the power vested in me... well, not really, but let's pretend," Fake Liberace said with a laugh. "I now pronounce you husband and wife... again."

"Mine," Sloan said.

"That's exactly what you said last time, too!" Fake Liberace clapped, but I had stopped paying attention to him when Sloan pulled me in for a sweet kiss, sealing our union... again. This time, we did it in front of our closest friends in a night no one would forget.

We marched down the aisle with Liberace on our heels. Sloan paused to give Elliott a smack on the back.

Liberace paused and glanced at Angela—tossing her an odd look with his eyebrows furrowed. Then he glanced at Elliott. Again, same look.

Then he snapped his fingers, smiled, and nodded like he knew something he wasn't supposed to share.

I made a mental note to ask Angela about that later. Then I mentally underlined it three times.

We headed to the after-party at the ARIA, where I'd reserved a four-tier cake and a pasta bar with all six kinds of sauces. I'd even booked a jazz band, like I'd always wanted for my wedding.

But Sloan paused in front of the M&M Store.

So much—so, so, so much—had happened since we saw the guy who played Tarzan here a year ago.

"Check out that fire margarita stand." T.J. pointed behind Sloan and me, wrecking the gentle moment of silence playing out between us.

I sucked in a breath.

It couldn't be the same stand.

No, that wasn't possible since the place had certainly been shut down at some point in the past year.

I turned to peek and, sure enough, the same stand with the same homemade signs and the same bartender still slinging the same yardstick drinks was right there.

T.J. started toward the stand like he would make a purchase we all knew he'd regret, but Sloan caught his arm.

"Nah, man, you don't want what he's selling." Sloan and I both shook our heads.

"Yeah, I do." T.J. tried to pull his arm away, but Sloan held tighter. "There's a souvenir cup."

"Let the man have his booze," Finn said, clearly not under-standing the importance of avoiding that vendor.

"I want one," T.J. whined.

"I promise you do not." Sloan shook his head.

T.J. pouted, but he made no more attempts to get to the margaritas.

Sloan wrapped his arm around my waist, and I returned the gesture.

Let the tabloids talk about our trip to Vegas tomorrow. No doubt, some would love it, and some would hate it, and I didn't care who said what because I had Sloan.

Sloan, who kissed me... right in front of the M&M Store there on the Vegas Strip.

People stared, and there were cameras, but I didn't care because I had him.

He was mine.

Enjoyed the story?
There's more Sloan and Maya in a
special bonus scene!

Grab your copy here:
christinahovland.com/onthemapbonus

ACKNOWLEDGMENTS

Thanks, as always, to my family: Steve and all four of our children for supporting me in this crazy job of mine.

Mom, thanks for giving me a writing cave to escape into and for handing out guitar picks at my signings.

Sereneti, thank you for always enjoying my stories and telling me so.

Thanks to those writer friends who keep me grounded: Dylann Crush, Serena Bell, Jody Holford, Brenda St. John Brown, Claire Marti, CR Grissom, AY Chao, Patricia Dane, Molly O'Hare, Gail Chianese, and so many others.

Thank you, as always, to my agent, Emily Sylvan Kim.

Karie you make me so happy. Thank you for being my bestie. The Thelma to my Louise… or vice versa. Whatever we decided.

Gretchen… what can I say? You're the bomb-dot-com. I'm so blessed you are in my life.

Gina, thanks for being my movie buddy and always having a listening ear.

My editorial team on this book went above and beyond. Thanks to Kristi Yanta, Cathy Yardley, Susan Soares, Audrey Nelson, L.A. Mitchell, and Shasta Shafer.

But the team's not complete there:

Anna Lee Kint, you are so amazing for always sending me your notes and thoughts so I can fix all the things! I appreciate you!

Beth Carbutt, as always, thanks for being my editorial goddess!

Suzie Waggoner, thank you for being my Typo Terminator.

Make no mistake, if you've found a typo in the book it's because I made a change after Suzie's thumbs up.

And thank *you*, yes YOU, for making my dream of being an author a reality. This is a pretty great job I've got!

The Mile High Matched Series

Rock Hard Cowboy, Mile High Matched, Book .5

Going Down on One Knee, Mile High Matched, Book 1

Blow Me Away, Mile High Matched, Book 2

Take It Off the Menu, Mile High Matched, Book 3

Do Me a Favor, Mile High Matched, Book 4

Ball Sacked, Mile High Matched, Book 4.5

Can't Believe You Came, Mile High Matched, Book 5 (*Coming Fall 2023*)

The Mile High Rocked Series

Played by the Rockstar, Mile High Rocked, Book 1

Knocked Up by the Rockstar, Mile High Rocked, Book 2

Married to the Rockstar, Mile High Rocked, Book 3

Tapped by the Rockstar, Mile High Rocked, Book 4

Reckless with the Rockstar, Mile High Rocked, Book 5

Mile High Stallions

In the Friend Zone (Coming Soon!)

Standalone Novel(s)

The Honeymoon Trap Confessions

It Doesn't Have to Be This Hard

The Mommy Wars Series

Rachel, Out of Office

There's Something About Molly

April May Fall

ABOUT THE AUTHOR

Christina Hovland lives her own version of a fairy tale—a retired artisan chocolatier turned romance writer. Born in Colorado, Christina received a degree in journalism from Colorado State University. Before opening her chocolate company, Christina's career spanned from the television newsroom to managing an award-winning public relations firm. She's a recovering over-achiever and perfectionist with a love of cupcakes and dinner she doesn't have to cook herself. A 2017 Golden Heart® finalist, she lives in Colorado with her first-boyfriend-turned-husband, four children, the sweetest dogs around, and Mayonnaise the wonder cat.

GET YOUR PLAYED ON!

**Turn the page for chapter one of
Played by the Rockstar!**

**He's a rock star.
She's a waitress.
He's about to rock her world.**

Certified behavioral counselor (and former band groupie) Becca Forrester needs a break. Taking a leave of absence from her job, she moves into the apartment over her parents' garage, and clinches a gig waitressing at a dive bar known for bringing in big name musicians.

Cedric "Linx" Lincoln is a certified rock star. Bassist for the hugely popular rock band, Dimefront, he's in Denver while the band is on hiatus a-freaking-gain. He's looking for something—anything—to keep him occupied until they can all get back to making music. When he saunters into his friend's bar, he finds the perfect diversion.

Becca's presence is a breath of fresh air. The sizzle she ignites in him is precisely what he needs. Bonus: no-stress, no-strings hookups are his specialty. But when things between them tip toward serious, his band implodes, and Becca's leave of absence ends, they're forced to decide what their "real" lives should look like. Maybe there's room for an encore...

CHAPTER ONE

BECCA

Neon beer signs totally signaled a new beginning. Sure, a girl might not think it possible, but Rebecca—Becca—Forrester was out to prove they could. The scent of hops and bourbon paired with the blast of music through the speakers and constant hum of life in the background at Brek's Bar in Denver, Colorado. Outside, the snow had turned to a slushy mess. Inside, the bar warmed her like she'd taken a shot of top-shelf whiskey.

Oh yes, this joint was the perfect place for a fresh start that did not involve anyone else or the baggage they dragged along with them.

"Why do you want to wait tables here?" Brek asked, giving a dose of emphasis on *here*. "I'd have thought you'd prefer some place with tablecloths."

Becca laughed. Brek was as biker as biker got—long hair, leather, and an abundance of tattoos. His wife was…not. She was a financial planner, and Becca's friend.

Becca shook her head. She definitely didn't want to wait tables anywhere else. "I'm looking for the diviest dive I can find."

The idea to wait tables was a complete one-eighty from her

203

recent past as a certified behavioral counselor, but she wouldn't go back. Not yet. Especially not when she was having a perfectly lovely time at the local go-to spot for great music in Denver, hanging with her friends, and harassing Brek into hiring her as a part-time waitress while she took a life break.

"Diviest dive? Well, I guess this is your place." Brek flashed her a smile.

"Exactly." Becca tucked a lock of her thick, brown hair behind her ear, where it belonged but never stayed. "Until I figure out what comes next for me."

"You can live the dream right here with me." Brek patted the bar top like it was a living, breathing thing. Something he adored.

Sigh. Someday she wanted someone to look at her like Brek looked at his wife and his bar top.

Not now. She was on a break from all of that—the relationships, the responsibility, everything—but, someday, the adoration thing would be fun to have, too.

He'd created the perfect dive bar atmosphere—neon lights on the dark wood over the bar with his name lit up in blue. The wood paneling covering the walls was new enough to make the place look well-kept but beat up enough that it didn't look like he had tried too hard. Aesthetically, nothing matched. Yet everything still worked together. The place was definitely Instagram-worthy.

The darkened room hopped in preparation for the band to take the stage. A vibe she loved pulsed through the air. That feeling right before music blasts and the lights come to life. Yep. This was exactly what she wanted for her present life: loud music and the familiar faces of the bar's regulars, with no further obligation for the mental or physical well-being for those around her.

Also, the best bands played at Brek's Bar. Sometimes, because he had the connections, Brek brought in huge names. Like *huuuge*. Waiting tables here was perfect for a recovering groupie on hiatus from life.

"You can start next weekend?" Brek asked.

"Next weekend would be perfection." Becca glanced at her friends, mingling across the room.

Then *Linx* entered Brek's Bar. Becca choked on nothing but air.

Linx. Walked. Through. The. Door.

Bassist for Dimefront. Hot as all hell. Heartbreak in leather pants when he took the stage.

She, on the other hand, was only hot when she wore a sweater. Definitely not heartbreak in any kind of clothing. Unless... Could a woman be heartbreak in yoga pants? She was sure that wasn't possible. She shook the thought from her head as he moved her direction.

Her mouth didn't just go dry; her entire body froze in time.

Tonight, he'd ditched the leather and wore shredded blue jeans instead. Lanky, with ridiculously long dark hair, stubble that was a half day away from being a full beard, and all the charisma of a man who could get tens of thousands of screaming fans on their feet with one chord on his guitar. He scanned the room like he owned the joint.

Brek may have owned the bar, but Linx owned the room.

"Looks like my current assignment is here," Brek said, offhand with a touch of growl.

"Linx is your assignment?" Okay, she tried to resist sliding her gaze back to Linx, but she failed. Every woman in the house got the Linx grin as he continued his slow saunter through the room.

"I'm his babysitter..." Brek said, glowering in Linx's general direction.

Crumpet crap-ola. Her blood seemed a whole lot thicker and her skin a whole lot thinner when he sauntered toward Brek... and her. The blue neon halo was a nice touch. Well done, universe. Well done, indeed.

She sighed because.... Linx.

All eyes were on him. Every woman in the room got a solid eye canoodle as he strutted right up to where she stood across from Brek. His eye canoodle could likely get a girl pregnant. She sucked in a breath and braced for her turn.

Linx moved less than an arms-length away, and her heart stuttered like he'd asked her to remove her panties. Surely, he wouldn't recognize her. It'd been years since they partied in the same circles.

She held her breath because she couldn't take the risk of his scent. Not because she had any special superpowers that involved scented rock stars—that she was aware of—but she knew he smelled amazing. Rock star heaven and concerts and something musky, like oak trees in the rain.

"Do you want me to wait for the drinks, or do you want to send them over when they're done?" Becca asked Brek, ignoring the fact that Linx was right-freaking-there doing some kind of intense handshake thing with him.

"You should definitely wait," Linx said, blasting her out of her knickers with that smile of his.

Yes, she often thought in British slang that she'd picked up one summer on a European Dimefront tour. She really took to their language choices. Refined, but still rather raunchy.

Like her. Rather, who she wanted to be.

She slid her gaze up the length of Linx—long and lithe. Not beefcake, but definitely built. He had more of a runner's build. Muscle and sinew, but not overdone.

He leaned against the bar top, a look of pure happiness on his face. This wasn't a cat's-got-his-cream smile. This was a cat's-about-to-play-with-his-dinner-before-devouring grin.

"Becca, this is Cedric," Brek said, slinging drinks like a pro.

Cedric?

Right. Sure, yes, she knew that was his given name. Cedric Sebastian, wasn't it? Last name was Lincoln, and all the original members of the band took a nickname that had an x at the end. Together, they made a triple-x, which they found hysterical, as pointed out in multiple Rolling Stone articles.

"Becca," Linx—er, *Cedric*—stretched her name across his tongue and played it like an instrument.

He held his hand out to her. *What to do? What to do?*

206

She could touch him. She should touch him. He was expecting her to touch him.

Do something already, Becca.

She was overthinking this way too much. So she gave him a solid handshake.

The way he squeezed her palm was nearly erotic. For no good reason, either. It was just a handshake. He didn't make any lewd gestures or anything.

Still, the bar seemed to zip to a pinprick and focus on Linx.

"Becca is a friend of Velma's." Brek tossed Linx a look like her dad used to give her when he thought she was going to use very poor decision-making skills.

Becca extracted her hand from Linx's grasp. She noted how he kept the touch for as long as she'd allow.

"I like Velma." Linx grabbed a pretzel from the bowl on the bar and flipped it into his mouth.

"I do, too." Brek continued working. "That's why I'm making it clear to you that *Becca* is a friend of *Velma's*. Which means stop looking at her like that."

"Like what?" Linx held up his hands.

"Like you want to make her Denver," Brek said with a growl.

What the heck did that mean?

Linx popped another pretzel into his mouth. Somehow, he chewed, smirked, and smoldered, all at the same time.

"She's not Denver. Denver is Denver. Becca is Becca."

Brek crossed his arms. "You and I need to discuss what you're allowed to do and not do while you're visiting."

Linx held his palm to his heart and wobbled dramatically. "I am offended."

For the record, he didn't sound offended.

"It's not visiting if I bought a house. That makes it my home," Linx said to Brek.

He bought a house in Denver? Huh.

Perhaps Becca wasn't the only one in the midst of reconsidering life choices.

"You *bought* a house in Denver?" Brek asked. "I thought it was a vacation rental."

"It was," Linx said with a shrug.

"The landlord was being a total dick about Gibson, so I made him an offer." Linx did the pretzel thing again.

"Who's Gibson?" Becca asked.

Not that she had any real reason to be part of the conversation, but Linx hadn't asked her to leave.

"His cat," Brek said, arms still crossed.

"He's more than a cat." Now Linx crossed his arms. "So what if I bought one little house so he has a place to live?"

Brek shook his head. "Whatever, man. You do you."

"That's my plan." Linx slid his gaze to Becca. "Unless Becca wants to sit here and have a drink with me? Then we can see what happens."

Linx gave her a charisma-soaked smile.

Ah. There it was, her eye canoodle. She felt that stare deep down in her soul.

Yeah. Total player.

A player who went through sex partners like they were potato chips. This was according to his bandmate, Bax, and general female knowledge when meeting a player of his magnitude.

Back when she'd followed Dimefront concerts she'd had her eye on Linx. Something about him was like a magnet, pulling her in his direction. She had wanted him. Full. Stop.

But Linx was bad news for her. He rocked a total love them and leave them vibe. The kind that made a girl like Becca— someone who tended to see only the good in people and, there-fore, fall for the wrong men—step away. He had just the right amount of baggage for her to want to unpack. And he was exactly the type of guy to pick up those suitcases and leave town right after she committed to the unpacking.

So she kept far away from his wandering gaze, preferring to observe him in his natural rock star habitat, and not let her heart, or body, get involved.

Brek handed a bottle of Coors to Linx.

"I've actually…" Becca jerked her head toward her group of friends. "Got to get back."

"That's a drag." Linx shrugged and gave Becca an extra-long, excessively thorough glance.

She shouldn't have done it. But she did. Yes, she totally canoodled him back.

"Becca?" Brek's voice cut through whatever the heck was going on between the two of them.

Brek had, of course, known Becca during her groupie days. Back then, he'd managed Dimefront and she'd been a Ten, the pet name they called their groupies. The Grateful Dead had Deadheads, Justin Bieber had his Beliebers, and Dimefront had their Tens. She'd spent a summer being Queen of the Tens.

This was not something she shared regularly. With anyone. No one else in her real life knew. Not even her best friends. That summer had been her first attempt at a life vacation. And it'd worked. Lucky for her, Brek didn't, and she was quoting here, "Broadcast shit that wasn't his to tell."

She let out a long breath and turned to Brek. He glanced pointedly to the order he'd prepared.

"Thanks." She snatched the remaining drinks and—and this was the hard part—she walked away without looking back at Linx and his neon halo.

Enjoyed the sample?
Played by the Rockstar is Available Now!

Played by the Rockstar